Tears blurred Reese's vision as the baby was placed in her waiting arms.

Until that moment he hadn't been completely hers. Now he was.

Tears spilled down her cheeks. During the past six years she had shed an ocean of tears. These were different. Cleansing. Healing. Welcome.

"Hello, my little one," she whispered. "Here you are at last."

She rocked on one foot and then the other, settling into a rhythm that was ages old and yet so new to her. "I know you," she murmured, awed by the powerful sense of connection and recognition she felt. "I would know you anywhere. You're my son."

More tears came, wetting her cheeks and washing away the old heartache. She looked up to see Duncan, and their gazes locked. She could have sworn his eyes, too, were glistening with unshed tears. What was *he* thinking? What was *he* feeling?

Dear Reader,

Anyone who's ever been on the infertility treadmill can attest to how tiring it is and what a toll it can take on even the strongest marriage. Turning to adoption is not an easy choice for many people, and doing so requires couples to first grieve the loss of the biological child they wanted to have.

Sometimes one spouse finishes that grieving process more quickly than the other. That's the case for Reese in *Their Very Special Gift*. Duncan also has doubts about whether he can love an adopted child. But babies are indeed a very special gift, and he soon learns what all adoptive parents know: love stretches far beyond biology when it comes to forming families.

I hope you enjoy reading Duncan and Reese's story.

Best wishes,

Jackie Braun

JACKIE BRAUN
Their Very Special Gift

Heart *to* Heart

HARLEQUIN®

TORONTO • NEW YORK • LONDON
AMSTERDAM • PARIS • SYDNEY • HAMBURG
STOCKHOLM • ATHENS • TOKYO • MILAN • MADRID
PRAGUE • WARSAW • BUDAPEST • AUCKLAND

For Jamie. We think of you often and are grateful to you always. And for Bonnie M., who so lovingly cared for our son until he came home.

ISBN-13: 978-0-373-18287-9
ISBN-10: 0-373-18287-2

THEIR VERY SPECIAL GIFT

First North American Publication 2007.

www.eHarlequin.com

Printed in U.S.A.

Jackie Braun on *Their Very Special Gift*

"Birth parents make an unimaginable sacrifice when they choose adoption. It's my hope that they find some consolation in knowing that their deepest heartache has become someone else's greatest joy."

Jackie Braun worked as an award-winning editorial writer before leaving her job at a daily newspaper to write romance. She is a two-time RITA® Award finalist, three-time National Readers' Choice Award finalist and a past winner of the Rising Star Award in traditional romance. She lives in Michigan, with her husband and son, and can be reached through her Web site: www.jackiebraun.com

PROLOGUE

REESE NEWCASTLE stood in the doorway of their home's master bedroom and watched her husband of seven years pack his suitcases. She'd seen him do this before— dozens of times in the past in fact, when his management position at the bank had required him to travel. But this was different. Duncan wasn't going to some seminar or conference or out-of-town meeting. No.

He was leaving her.

His movements were economical despite being jerky from what she recognized as barely suppressed anger. It was the only emotion of his that she seemed to be able to identify readily these days, even though once upon a time she had known the meaning of his every gesture and glance.

In no time at all he had emptied the

contents of his bureau drawers into one of the
two large suitcases that were spread open on
their queen-size bed. Reese frowned at what
she could see of the rumpled poppy-print
comforter.

When was the last time they had slept in
that bed together? When was the last time
they'd made love or simply touched one
another in kindness or affection? She
couldn't remember. Even their last civil conversation seemed a distant memory.

She rubbed her arms briskly through the
wool turtleneck sweater she wore, feeling
chilled. More than cold, she felt sick and
scared and horribly, horribly hurt as the only
sounds that broke the silence were the scrape
and slide of empty drawers as Duncan
shoved them closed with his knee.

The days and weeks of their ongoing
cold war ran together in an indiscernible
blur. Yet even now—as her husband
prepared to move out and her broken heart
shattered into even smaller, more jagged
pieces—Reese's pride kept her from
offering an olive branch. She could not
forgive him.

He was having an affair.

Oh, he'd denied at first, acting wounded and offended that she would even make such an accusation. The second, third and fourth times she'd brought it up also were met with vehement protestations of innocence. But tonight, when he'd arrived home late yet again and Reese had confronted him with her suspicions that his friendliness with the bank's sexy new vice president went beyond either the professional or the platonic, he had not dismissed her claims of infidelity. No. He'd stared at her in stony silence, his expression an odd combination of anger and what seemed to be defeat.

Deny it, she'd begged silently.

But he hadn't. Instead he'd gone to the attic to retrieve his luggage. As far as Reese was concerned, he'd waved the white flag of surrender when he'd begun packing his bags. It was clear to her. He'd found someone else.

He stalked past her now to the room's spacious walk-in closet. She heard a rustling of metal hangers accompanied by a few grumbled oaths. When he came out a moment later he had an armful of tailored shirts, which he shoved into the second suitcase, tucking them into every available corner without bothering to fold them.

"Your clothes are going to wrinkle," she murmured absently.

Duncan stopped what he was doing and turned, glaring at her from beneath a slash of dark brows. The opaque blue eyes that had once lit up with mischief or merriment were as cold and remote as a shark's.

"That's what you're worried about right now? You're worried about my damned clothes?" He didn't wait for her to answer before he added, "Well, don't lose sleep over it, Reese. I'm sure there will be an iron where I'm going."

"Breanna Devin's?" She spat out the vice president's name as if it were rotten fruit.

As she studied his face for clues, she thought she saw his jaw clench briefly, but once again he didn't deny anything. Instead he disappeared into the closet a second time. When he came out afterward he was holding half a dozen business suits, which he threw into the suitcase hangers and all.

"I guess I can understand the attraction. She probably has perfectly functioning ovaries," Reese muttered.

Duncan whirled to face her. "God! That's all you think about! I swear for the past six years you've had a one-track mind. Babies, babies, babies!"

"You want a baby, too."

"I want…" His voice trailed off and he shook his head. The spark of anger she'd witnessed was momentarily snuffed out. Was that resignation that took its place? "Never mind what I want."

"You want a biological child," Reese supplied anyway. "You want a baby who shares your genes." Her voice broke despite her best intentions when she added, "A baby I cannot have with you."

"Reese."

He lifted one hand, almost as if reaching for her.

It fell to his side when she added, "But now you've found someone who can."

Maybe she should have expected that he would look elsewhere. Medically the problem was hers. *She* was the reason they were childless. *She* was the reason they had stopped trying.

Duncan had been pretty vocal in his opinion that they should continue with fertility treatments, despite the fact that the last two procedures had resulted in pregnancies that had ended in miscarriage. They'd both been devastated, but Duncan had not been deterred. A specialist in Chicago was having luck with difficult cases such as theirs, according to their doctor. Duncan had pleaded with Reese to go see the man, but she had refused.

Didn't he understand? she'd wondered at the time. Couldn't he see that she'd had enough? Couldn't he see that her heart was too broken, her body too abused to endure more hormone injections, more egg retrievals and embryo transfers, especially when carrying a pregnancy to term seemed to be beyond her ability?

Adoption was their solution, their salvation, she'd told him. And so almost two years ago she'd talked him into making an appointment at a local agency that specialized in domestic infant placements. When they'd filled out the application, Reese had felt a measure of control and peace that she hadn't experienced in years. Not since before she'd bought a basal thermometer a week after their first wedding anniversary and had begun to chart her ovulation cycles.

Duncan's enthusiasm had never matched her own, even though he had dutifully attended the education classes with her and met with the counselor assigned to do their home study.

Then, one night as they had sat at the kitchen table selecting family photographs to put in the portfolio that birth mothers would view at the agency to help them pick adoptive parents for their babies, he'd asked quietly: "What if I can't love a child who's not really mine?"

His concern had shaken Reese to the core, but she'd dismissed it quickly. Fear had forced her to.

"Of course you can. You will." She'd smiled brightly even as his brows had tugged together with worry.

Who couldn't love a baby, whether it was biologically related to him or not?

Even if Duncan *thought* he couldn't love an adopted child, she'd been sure that once he held their baby in his arms all of his misgivings would disappear.

But as their wait for word from the agency had dragged on and the strain began to take its toll on their marriage, Reese had been forced to face the painful truth: Duncan's support for taking this alternative pathway to parenthood was begrudging at best. More likely, he had manufactured it entirely for her benefit.

Now, his words underscored those facts.

"Yes, I want a biological child. I've never made a secret of that. I thought we should have at least met with the doctor in Chicago before giving up. But do you know what I want more than a child?"

More than a child? Reese frowned.

"I want a wife who is as interested in having a husband as she is in starting a family."

The words landed like flaming arrows, searing her already wounded heart. It was not guilt, she told herself, that had her snapping, "So, my preoccupation excuses the fact you've turned to someone else?"

He closed his eyes briefly, shook his head and sighed. "If you believe that it must be true. God knows, you're never wrong about anything, are you, Reese?"

Prove me wrong. She wanted to shout it. Instead she crossed her arms over her chest, tipped up her chin and said nothing.

"If you need to reach me, call my cell or call the office. I'll be back later in the week while you're at work to get the rest of my clothes and pick up my mail."

"Where are you going?"

His lips twisted as he zipped closed the bags. "Can't you guess? I thought you had all the answers."

A bubble of panic rose like bile in her throat. "If you go to her now, don't come back to me."

Duncan jerked the bags off the bed and started for the doorway, forcing Reese to retreat into the hall.

I love you. Don't leave.

She swallowed the plea, though, as he strode past her. Her heart beat in time with the clipped cadence of his footsteps on the hardwood floor. Instead the words that slipped through her trembling lips were: "I want a divorce."

His stride hitched and for a moment he stopped. He stood with his back to her. God, how she wished she could catch even a glimpse of his face so she could try to gauge his reaction. Just beyond his left shoulder, hanging on the wall, she could see a framed photograph of the two of them. It had been taken while they were on their honeymoon in Hawaii and in it he was smiling adoringly at her. Their past happiness mocked her now as Duncan once again started down the hall without acknowledging her request.

Reese rushed after him. She followed him out into the frigid January night and then stood in her stocking feet on the frozen brick pavers that led from the front porch to the driveway of their Grosse Pointe home in metropolitan Detroit.

"Did you hear me, Duncan?" Her voice rose shrilly as she repeated with a conviction she did not feel. "I said I want a divorce."

This time, the hateful words didn't so much as slow him. He kept going until he reached his car, where he hefted the heavy bags into the trunk, slammed it shut with unnecessary force and then walked to the driver's side door.

Reese's ragged breath turned white and hovered in front of her face a brief second before the wind snatched it away. All of her hope seemed to go with it. As she stood, shivering and miserable in their front yard, Duncan got into the car, gunned the engine to life and drove away.

CHAPTER ONE

Two weeks later...

DUNCAN shifted his Mercedes into Park and switched off the ignition, but he made no move to get out. He stared at the ranch with its charming red brick facade and canvas-awning-covered windows. The place wasn't big. In fact, at twenty-five hundred square feet, it was the smallest one-story in their tasteful, older Grosse Pointe neighborhood. But he'd always liked the inviting look of it. Unlike his parents' mammoth Lakeshore Drive estate, this place had seemed like a home.

Not any longer, of course. No. Now it was just a house.

What am I doing here?

For the millionth time he wondered why

he hadn't refused to come back, why he hadn't just said no when Reese had asked for his help. The answer he kept coming up with was not one he liked.

He still loved her.

Even though she had broken his heart with her accusations and had pushed him away with her single-minded obscssion over the past several years, he still loved her. And so he was back, not as her husband but as her means to an end.

The adoption agency had called. A birth mother had picked the Newcastles as parents for her baby. Reese, of course, was elated, ecstatic even, and, not surprisingly, desperate. Neither the folks at Loving Hands Adoption nor the young mother knew that the Newcastles were living apart, their marriage in such shambles that they were heading for divorce. Reese had never notified their caseworker and Duncan certainly hadn't thought to call Jenny Lawford after he'd moved out on that bleak January night.

Hell, he hadn't told anyone that he and Reese were having problems, let alone considering calling it quits. He hadn't said a word to his parents or his friends. Even his secretary didn't know he was sleeping at a hotel, taking his meals at restaurants or ordering them through room service. Why broadcast failure? It wasn't, Duncan told himself, that he'd been holding out hope for reconciliation.

Of course, if he had been, Reese's proposal of the day before would have pretty much snuffed out that possibility. She'd dropped by his office unexpectedly in the late afternoon, and, he could admit, he'd been happy to see her…right up until the point she'd revealed the actual reason for her visit. She'd told him about the agency's call and then she'd asked him to move home.

She needed him to pretend that everything was fine for the six months or so it would take until the adoption petition was finalized in family court. After that, they would go before a judge again—this time for their divorce. In return for his help in securing the adoption she'd promised to cut him loose quickly and cleanly.

As Duncan sat in his car he rubbed a hand over his eyes, remembering how Reese had offered that up like some kind of damned grand prize.

"I'll make the divorce easy for you afterward," she'd said. "I won't ask for anything but what I came into our marriage with. It goes without saying that I won't expect you to pay child support or have a relationship with the child in any way. I know how you feel about adoption."

Now she knew? Before, every time he'd tried to broach the subject, she'd cut him off or dismissed his concerns. He'd stared at her, wondering how it was possible for two people to talk to one another and yet fail to communicate. Not surprisingly, she'd taken his silence to mean something else entirely.

"You can even have the house."

"I don't want the damned house," he'd told her. Had she really believed it would sweeten the deal to throw in the deed to the place where he'd once known such joy?

"Then what do you want? Name it and I'll give it to you." God, she'd been so eager in her desperation that it had made his heart ache all the more. "This might be my last chance, Duncan. I'm begging you."

It hadn't escaped his notice that she didn't use the more inclusive "our" in referring to chances. And, in fairness, why would she? Adoption was *her* answer to their reproductive problems. He'd never accepted it as their solution. He'd never given up on the idea of a biological child. He still wasn't sure he could feel for a baby what he should feel if the child wasn't of his blood.

"You could apply as a single mother," he'd reminded her, his gut clenching over the words. "There was an unmarried woman in the education classes we had to attend. Or you could hire an attorney and go the private route."

"I know. I know."

She'd looked so weary then and he'd understood why. Private adoption held its own set of perils, which was why they had ruled it out from the onset. Birth mothers could change their minds after expenses had been paid and after infants had been placed, and adoptive families had no recourse.

As for their agency, because it was so small it only allowed singles to adopt special-needs children or those who have been removed from their biological parents' homes for abuse or neglect.

"I want *this* baby, Duncan," Reese had said. "I'm thirty-six, looking at thirty-seven in June. All of my friends are mothers. Even my younger sister is expecting. I can't keep waiting. I just can't. It's been so long already."

Her voice had broken and her eyes had filled. Duncan had known right then what his answer would be. He'd always hated to see her cry. It made him feel powerless, inadequate. As they'd stood in the sterile confines of his downtown Detroit office, it had reminded him of the many ways in which he already had failed her. He was a man of action, a mover and shaker adept at making deals, at making things happen. Why, *why* couldn't he find a way to fix their fertility problem?

Sighing now, he thought, maybe I owe her. Maybe, after everything she's gone through—physically, mentally and emotionally—in their quest for a biological child, she deserves this chance.

He didn't know. The only thing that was clear was that he'd loved but one woman in his life and, even though he was losing her, even though she'd made it clear that their marriage was as good as over, he wanted her to be happy. Maybe then he could move on and find, if not happiness for himself, at least a measure of peace. He certainly didn't have either now.

The front door opened and Reese stepped out onto the porch. Other than yesterday, it was the first time Duncan had seen her in a couple of weeks. She looked pretty much the same as she always had, which meant she still managed to steal his breath. Studying her closer, though, he decided she was a little thinner than she had been before. Her high cheekbones seemed more pronounced, her chin slightly more pointed. Her wavy hair, a deep honey color shot through with chunky golden highlights, was scraped back into its usual messy ponytail, giving him an unfettered view of her expression. There were shadows under her brown eyes and he thought he saw questions in them. More than anything, though, he recognized gratitude in the nervous bowing of her lips.

Gratitude.

Swallowing a sigh, he got out of the car and walked up the brick-paver path he'd helped her lay the second summer they'd owned the house. At the time, he'd wanted to hire out the job. She'd insisted they could do it themselves, though, and they had, which explained why one side of it sloped toward the street. Reese had always claimed that imperfection gave it character. She'd been good at that, finding the positive where others saw only negatives. And she'd been good at talking him into doing things that were beyond his experience as well as outside of his comfort zone—his return now being a case in point.

Somehow, though, Duncan doubted that this time when their collaboration was through he was going to feel the same odd sense of accomplishment he had with the pavers.

He stopped just before the porch. She tucked her hands into the back pockets of her jeans and canted one long leg to the side. The pose made her seem younger. It reminded him of the way she'd looked when they'd met nearly a decade before, except now she wasn't eyeing him with that frank appreciation he'd always found so damned arousing.

No. Gratitude, he thought again.

"Hello, Duncan. Thanks for coming."

"Reese." He nodded stiffly.

"I…I was getting worried that you'd changed your mind." Nervous laughter punctuated her words.

"Traffic," he lied. The truth was he'd driven past their street three times before finally turning down it.

God, what a painful and awkward farce this was. That feeling only intensified when she reminded him, "Jenny called a few minutes ago. She's running a little behind schedule, but she said she should be here in about an hour."

Their caseworker from the adoption agency was coming to discuss the timetable for moving the baby from foster care to the Newcastles' residence. At least, that's what Duncan recalled from his conversation with Reese the day before. Maybe there was more to it than that. He couldn't say. He hadn't made an effort to commit the details to memory, perhaps because in the long run none of this really involved him. He was just a prop, a necessary accessory—at least for the interim.

He nodded again. "An hour."

"Yes. Four o'clock. The home inspection she's doing for a client in St. Clair Shores is taking a little more time than she anticipated." Reese glanced past him to his car and inquired politely, "Do you need help with your bags?"

"No. I can get them." He'd carried them out without any assistance. He could carry them back in.

He went to retrieve them and when he returned she was holding open the door. For a moment Duncan allowed himself to pretend he'd just been away on business and was now coming home, welcomed back… missed. The fantasy ended abruptly once they were inside. After taking his overcoat and hanging it in the foyer closet, Reese motioned toward the first door in the hallway that led away from the living room.

"You can put your bags in the guest room. We can determine who sleeps where later."

Who sleeps where.

"Sure." He shrugged. "Whatever."

He put the luggage on the floor next to the double bed. The mattress was lumpy. He knew that because he'd slept on it more than a few times during the months before moving out. When he turned, he spied Reese in the open doorway. She was eyeing the bed, too, and frowning. Then her gaze connected with his and she moistened her lips.

"I…I have one request to make," she said quietly.

"A request?" Duncan folded his arms over his chest. He knew that tone. He knew that look. And so he figured he knew exactly what was coming next. Bitterness had him asking, "Do you really think you're in any position right now to be making requests, Reese?"

"No." She lifted her chin and he saw her swallow. "But I'm making one anyway."

That was Reese, he thought, never short on nerve. Once upon a time, he'd admired that quality. Right now he resented the hell out of it.

"What?" He prompted her to continue with a jerky nod.

"I want you to promise me that you won't…that you won't *see* her until the adoption is final."

He figured "see" was a polite euphemism for "have sex with" since Duncan ran into the woman in question on a daily basis at his workplace.

"And after that?" he challenged as the old anger bubbled to the surface. He didn't bother to correct her assumptions about his relationship with Breanna Devin. After all, he knew what a pointless exercise that was. "What about after the adoption is final?"

"After that I…I…" As her words trailed away something flickered briefly in her expression. Something vulnerable and soft and in direct contrast to the hard set of her mouth.

"Do you have a problem with it then, Reese? Will you care then?" he goaded.

She cleared her throat. "After the adoption is final whatever you decide to do and whomever you decide to see will be your own business."

"Ah. How very accommodating of you," he drawled, unable to completely dismiss the disappointment he felt, but then what had he expected?

"I'm asking a lot," she admitted.

"You have no idea." He tugged off his tie

and tossed it onto the bed. Then he struggled with the top button of his shirt. Anger made his progress clumsy.

"Do you love her?"

His fingers stilled and he glanced at her sharply, an oath scraped his throat before escaping to echo in the room. "What do you think?"

A full minute ticked by as they stared at one another in rigid silence. It was a hollow victory that she was the first one to look away.

"Well, I'll let you get settled," she said at last.

When Reese turned to leave, Duncan couldn't stop himself from asking, "So, you'll accept my promise now? If I give you my word, you'll believe me?"

She regarded him solemnly over one shoulder before her chin lowered in a nod.

"Why, Reese?"

"What do you mean?" She was frowning as she turned to face him fully.

"What's changed? My promises, my *word*, they weren't good enough for you before."

"Duncan, you were, you *are* having an—"

He shook his head and interrupted. "No. It's not about me. It's *never* been about me, Reese. It's about you and the fact that after seven years of marriage you don't trust me."

He watched her blink, heard her swift intake of breath. No doubt she was gearing up for her rebuttal and it was bound to be a good one. She was a champion debater— another trait he'd once admired but now found damned tiring. He didn't want to hear her justifications for accusing him so unjustly. And so before she could open her mouth, Duncan stepped to the door and closed it in her face.

Duncan's rude dismissal surprised Reese, but no more so than his accusation.

You don't trust me.

No, she didn't—and for good reason. She was tempted to bang her fist on the door and remind him of that fact. What would it change, though? What would her anger, as reasonable and justified as it was, accomplish now that it hadn't accomplished in the past? She sighed, knowing the answer. Nothing. Absolutely nothing.

Besides, Jenny Lawford would be here soon. Reese needed Duncan. She couldn't afford to alienate him. She couldn't afford to have him rethinking his agreement to move home and help her. Of course, he'd been eager to do so since it meant he would be rid of her afterward, unfettered and utterly free to pursue his relationship with Breanna. Well, Reese told herself, she didn't care.

I'm going to be a mom. Finally I'm going to have a baby to love and nurture.

That was the most important thing. That was all that mattered. She ignored an insistent inner voice that kept turning those statements into questions.

Was that the most important thing?
Was that all that mattered?

If there was one thing Reese had learned during her seven years as a Newcastle, it was how to entertain with flair and style and to make one's guests feel welcome. Not that their caseworker was stopping by on a social call. Still, Reese had felt the occasion called for some refreshments, if only so she would have something to occupy her hands as she and Duncan sat together in their cozy living room and pretended to be the picture of wedded bliss.

On the low coffee table, right next to a vase full of fresh cut flowers she'd picked up at a florist shop, Reese set out a pot of hot tea, cups and saucers, linen napkins and plates for the finger sandwiches that were tastefully arranged on an heirloom silver platter.

Of course, Duncan didn't drink tea and thinly sliced cucumbers on buttered rye bread had never appealed to his palate, but as her mother-in-law, Louise Newcastle, had insisted on more than one occasion, appearances were what counted when one entertained.

Today that was true more than ever.

Reese couldn't stop herself from wondering what her prickly mother-in-law was going to make of this most recent turn of events. The woman had never made a secret of the fact she didn't find Reese suitable daughter-in-law material. Reese was too liberal, too opinionated and far too, well, common. She came from solidly blue-collar stock whereas Duncan was the scion of an old-money family that could trace its roots clear back to the Mayflower.

"Who are your people, dear?"

The woman had actually asked Reese that the first time Duncan had brought her home to meet his parents.

"My people?" she'd blinked. And if she hadn't already felt out of place having dinner in the Newcastles' formal dining room surrounded by more silverware than she knew what to do with, she certainly would have then.

"Reese's family lives back East," Duncan had said between spoonfuls of lobster bisque. "In Boston."

It had been pride that had Reese adding in her thickest Southie accent, "They're in hospitality services. My dad and his brother own Dandy's Pub. It's been in the family for two whole generations."

Louise Newcastle had gone as pale as her tennis whites. It wasn't to be the last time. No, Reese figured she'd managed to shave about a dozen years off the woman's life simply by being who she was. And who she was wasn't good enough for Louise's only son.

Louise had disapproved of Reese's choice of wedding dress. "It's too simple. Too... ordinary."

She'd disapproved of the quaint house the newlyweds had purchased. "You're going to live here?"

And she'd disapproved of the fact that Reese had opted to continue working as a high school art teacher after marriage rather than giving up her job and dedicating herself to lunching at the club. "Have you at least considered applying for a post at a private school?"

Then, when it had become clear that Reese and Duncan might never have what most couples took for granted, her mother-in-law's meddling and snide comments had become intolerable.

Reese still winced when she recalled the older woman's reaction upon learning that her daughter-in-law had talked Duncan into looking outside the Newcastle gene pool for an heir. As usual, her Palm Beach tan had bleached away, but this time, for the first time ever, Reese had heard the woman raise her voice.

"You're going to adopt? But what about that doctor you told me about in Chicago? That seemed so promising. I thought you were going to keep trying?"

She'd directed her questions to Duncan, who'd shaken his head. His jaw had been clenched and something akin to grief had shadowed his eyes. Louise Newcastle had shifted her gaze to Reese then and her accusing expression had made words unnecessary. Reese knew exactly what the older woman was thinking: Newcastles did not adopt. They had never needed to adopt... until Reese and her defective reproductive tract had come into the picture.

As if Reese hadn't felt like enough of a failure.

She shoved aside the memories as well as the old guilt. When Duncan entered the living room a few minutes later, she was crouched down in front of the fireplace, trying to coax a flame from a small stack of kindling. It was her third attempt and it appeared to be as successful as her previous two.

"Let me," he offered, kneeling next to her and taking the long matchstick from her hand. Humor, as wispy as the smoke curling from the twigs, sounded in his voice when he added, "You never could build a proper fire without making the entire house smell like smoke."

"I'm not as good at making things burn as you are," she agreed.

The double entendre had Duncan glancing at her in surprise. It was so reminiscent of the way they used to tease one another, but she hadn't meant it that way.

Even so, she thought she heard him murmur, "Oh, I don't know about that."

He struck the match against the hearth's bricks. It wasn't the only thing that seemed to flare with heat. Reese decided to change the subject. Or, rather, resurrect the one that had been bothering her.

"Have you decided what you are going to tell your parents?" she asked.

"What do you mean?"

"Well, I assume they know you moved out

and that we were…that we will be divorcing." She tucked a stray lock of hair behind one ear. "Now you're home and a baby is coming into the picture. They're bound to have questions. So, what will you tell them?"

Duncan leaned toward the hearth and blew gently on the wood. A small flame flickered and then shot up. He added more kindling before turning to face her.

"About the baby or about us?"

"Either. Both."

"It's really none of their business."

Reese frowned. "But they know you moved out, right?"

He shrugged, glanced away. "It's never come up."

Reese wasn't sure what to make of his answer. It certainly wasn't the response she'd expected from a man who was having an affair, a man who had been living elsewhere for a couple of weeks. It still bugged her that she didn't know exactly where that was.

"What…what about now? What will you say to them now?"

His voice was rife with impatience when

he replied, "I told you, it's none of their business."

"Come on, Duncan. I know how your mother feels about adoption and even your father never seemed overly thrilled with the idea."

Of course, unless it had to do with golf, the stock market or his alma mater's football team, Grayson Newcastle rarely offered an opinion on anything.

"So?"

"They won't accept this baby."

"They won't need to," he replied baldly.

"No. I guess not." She felt sad suddenly. Still, Duncan's blasé attitude was perplexing. "But none of that changes the fact that this baby will be a Newcastle."

"You're a Newcastle." His voice was soft and seemed to be laced with challenge. "As we both know, that doesn't mean anything. It's just a last name, easily used and discarded, isn't it?"

"Not to your mother."

She had him there.

His lips twisted. "No. Not to my mother." Then he sighed and walked to the large picture window, where he stood with his legs braced apart and his hands tucked into his front pockets. He'd changed from the tailored charcoal suit that was fitting attire for the bank president he was into a pair of khaki trousers and a button-down oxford. Even dressed casually he managed to appear put-together and polished thanks to his aristocratic good looks.

Reese had been put off by those looks at first, she recalled. Too sophisticated, too cultured. Too handsome—it turned out there was such a thing. The dark, nearly black hair. The sky-blue eyes. The slightly flared nose. The square jaw and chin with its movie-star dent. Add broad shoulders, slim hips and nicely muscled chest to the mix and Duncan Newcastle was a breathtaking example of male perfection.

Truthfully Reese had never quite known what he'd seen in her. Oh, she was attractive in a nontraditional sort of way with her untamed hair, freckle-dusted nose and slightly off-center smile. But she didn't delude herself into thinking she was pretty let alone classically beautiful like some of the women he'd dated before her. Women who belonged to his parents' club. Women who never had to think carefully about which fork to use for their salads.

Women like Breanna Devin.

"We're such an odd couple," she remarked.

Duncan turned, his dark eyebrows rising. "Why do you say that?"

She hadn't meant to, especially right now, even though she'd thought it often enough in the past. She shrugged. "Just thinking aloud. You know me."

"I used to think I did."

Yes, she'd thought so, too. She'd thought he'd understood her perfectly, just as she'd thought she'd understood him. Then infertility had come along like a gargantuan thundercloud on the horizon. It had blotted out every last bit of normalcy from their marriage. In the end, it turned out they didn't know one another at all.

"We're very different people," she murmured. She used to think that was the reason for their great chemistry. Opposites attracting. Yin to yang. Now she wasn't so sure. "Too different, I guess."

"Too different?" He pulled a hand from his pocket and massaged the back of his neck for a moment before tugging at the dark hair that brushed his collar. It was a familiar gesture, what she'd always thought of as Duncan's "thinking pose." After a long pause, he tucked his hand back into his pocket. "I guess maybe you're right."

Why did it hurt so much that he agreed with her?

Before she could come up with an answer, he announced, "Jenny's here."

CHAPTER TWO

"Hi, Mommy."

Jenny Lawford's delighted laughter rang out after she offered the greeting. Then she declared, "This is the best part of my job. You can't imagine how much I love finally being able to say that to you."

"Not as much as I love hearing it," Reese replied truthfully. Her heart was thumping wildly in her chest and her hands had turned clammy from a combination of nerves and excitement.

The other woman grinned broadly as she stepped into the Newcastles' foyer and unwound the fuzzy knitted scarf from around her neck. Jenny had mousey-brown hair and stood half a head shorter than Reese. She was a good decade younger, too, but her overall competence and self-assurance at times made her seem like an older, wiser sister.

She had a knack for putting other people at ease, offering sympathy rather than pity, and giving comfort laced with her signature good humor. On more than a few occasions during their acquaintance she had helped shore up Reese's flagging spirits with a few well-chosen words. Today, of course, no such effort was required. Reese's spirits were flying high…right along with her stress level.

Reese wasn't a deceitful person by nature. In fact, she prided herself on her honesty and integrity, but she ignored her throbbing conscience. She was determined to do everything within her power to ensure that when Jenny left she had no inkling that the Newcastles' marriage was in trouble. Surely the end in this case justified the means.

This might be my last chance.

She'd said as much to Duncan…*Duncan*. Her heart thumped again. So much depended on him.

He was crouched down before the hearth adding another log to the fire when they entered the living room. The picture he presented was so inviting, so painfully nostalgic, that Reese found herself wanting to believe he was home for good and happy to be there. But of course he wasn't. He stood, dusting his palms together. Then he crossed to them and held out a hand to Jenny.

"It's good to see you," he said in what Reese thought of as his formal banker's voice.

She felt some of the moment's warmth ebb away. He seemed so reserved just then, so much like his mother. *Loosen up!* she wanted to shout. *Do you have to look so grim?* He was acting as if he was about to foreclose on an elderly widow's house rather than hear exciting news about a long-awaited baby.

Reese glanced at Jenny in apprehension. Thankfully the other woman didn't seem put off.

"Hi. It's good to see you, too." Jenny's smile bloomed again when she winked and added, "Daddy."

Duncan's gaze shot to Reese and he flushed with what she hoped Jenny would interpret as delight rather than the trepidation it appeared to be.

"Here, let me take your coat," he offered, stepping behind Jenny to help her out of it.

When in turmoil Duncan always retreated behind good manners. Well, at least when he went to hang it in the foyer closet, Reese had the opportunity to explain, "He's a little nervous. I guess we both are."

"There's no need to be nervous. This baby isn't going to be snatched back." Jenny grinned.

Reese swallowed hard and gripped her hands together so tightly that her knuckles turned white.

If only she could be so certain. The fact remained, though, that if the Newcastles proved to be unsuitable parents for any reason at any point during the next six months, the baby would be removed from their care and the adoption would not go through. Heading for divorce surely fell under the "unsuitable" umbrella.

During their education classes they'd been told that such an occurrence happened only rarely. Slim though that chance was, Reese figured it still put most adoptive parents on edge. That was especially true in her situation, since she was trying to keep all evidence of her crumbling marriage from tumbling out into view.

"Please, have a seat." She unclasped her soggy hands long enough to wave in the general direction of the couch and chairs that were arranged in front of the fireplace. "I made hot tea and finger sandwiches."

"Oh, you didn't have to go to any trouble," Jenny admonished, but then her laughter boomed. "I'm really glad you did, though. It's been a crazy day and I haven't even had a chance to stop for lunch. I'm famished."

"Then help yourself," Reese coaxed.

Jenny settled into an overstuffed chair on the opposite side of the table while Reese perched on the edge of the sofa. She wanted to grab the younger woman by the shoulders and shake her until she had divulged every scrap of information she knew about the baby. Instead Reese pasted on a staid smile that would have done her mother-in-law proud and played the gracious hostess, nudging the tray of sandwiches closer to her guest's side of the table.

Jenny didn't reach for a sandwich, though.

She balanced her battered brown leather case on her knees and pulled out a file folder. Duncan had just returned when she said, "I thought you two might like to see a picture of your son."

"Son." Duncan dropped down onto the cushion next to Reese. She stole a glance at him and though his expression gave little away, from the corner of her eye she saw his Adam's apple bob. Twice.

Was he remembering?

She couldn't recall if she'd mentioned the sex of the baby when she'd talked to him yesterday. Jenny had given Reese few details during their phone conversation, but the baby's gender had been one of them. Still, boy or girl, it hadn't mattered to Reese. It had never mattered. She'd always just prayed for healthy. Duncan, however, had wanted a son. Oh, he'd claimed not to have a preference one way or the other, but Reese still remembered the way he'd kissed her flat belly after her first pregnancy was confirmed through a blood test at the fertility clinic.

"If it's a boy, I'd like to call him Daniel," he'd said.

It was the name of his best friend, who'd died of an inoperable brain tumor. The best friend who had introduced Reese and Duncan at a party because he thought they would "perfect" for one another.

Thinking of that first pregnancy now, Reese recalled how excited they'd been and how giddy with relief since the previous three rounds of fertility treatments had yielded no results. Six weeks later, when she'd begun spotting and cramping, they'd realized how naïve they'd been to believe a positive pregnancy test was where heartache ended and happily ever after began. Their second pregnancy had lasted nearly five months, long enough to build up their hopes before brutally dashing them again.

Finally parenthood seemed to be within their grasp. *My* grasp, she amended. Her husband, soon-to-be-ex-husband, wasn't really part of this.

She reached for the file at the same time Duncan did. Their fingers brushed and then their gazes collided. For the briefest moment she saw something in his blue eyes that buoyed her heavy heart. But then his hand fell away and even though he leaned closer to see when she flipped open the folder, she decided his interest was manufactured for Jenny's benefit.

Then it didn't matter. Her attention was riveted to the photograph that was clipped to the top of a sheet of paper detailing vital statistics.

"Oh…oh, my."

Tears threatened to blur her vision, but she blinked them back. She needed to see the baby clearly. She wanted to memorize every last detail of the little face that stared back at her from the picture.

She recognized the shot as the kind taken in a hospital nursery, which meant the baby was probably mere hours old. She knew a moment of regret. I wish I could have been there, she thought. I wish I could have heard his first cry, been the first one to hold him, offer comfort and welcome him into the world.

He was wearing a little blue knit cap, so it was impossible to tell what color his hair might be or even if he had any, but the eyes in his round face were deep blue and opened wide. He was wrapped in a pastel-hued receiving blanket, but he'd managed to work his arms free. The hands on both were balled into fists, which rested just below his chin.

"Oh, just look at him," Reese whispered to no one in particular. "He's so…he's so…"

Words failed her. She pressed her knuckles against her trembling lips and shook her head in wonder. It came as a surprise when Duncan finished her thought.

"He's perfect."

He sounded baffled. Duncan figured that made sense since that was exactly how he felt as he stared at the photograph. He'd never allowed himself to imagine what a nonbiological child would look like, but he recognized now the prejudice he'd felt.

It shamed him to realize he'd assumed an adopted baby would be inferior, probably sickly looking and perhaps even a little homely. After all, who would give up a healthy and handsome child? Hadn't his mother suggested as much? But this baby was beautiful and oddly familiar. It was a trick of the light, an illusion created by the camera lens, not to mention an utter impossibility, but Duncan swore he saw Reese's stubborn chin represented in that tiny face, and her coloring in the pale skin. Even the fighter pose seemed to mimic her plucky personality.

"He looks like you," he whispered, shaken.

Reese blinked at him, but Jenny took his incongruous comment in stride.

"You know, I thought so, too," she agreed. "That seems to happen a lot, even when the birth parents don't play any role in picking the adoptive families. No one really knows why. One of those weird coincidences. Just wait until he gets older and learns your mannerisms and parrots your voice inflections. Perfect strangers will come up to you in restaurants or the grocery store to tell you how much alike you are."

I won't be around then, Duncan thought. Beside him, Reese shifted in her seat, crossing and then uncrossing her legs. Was she thinking that, too?

"Well, you must have questions," Jenny said after a moment. "Lots of them. So, fire away." She smiled knowingly and settled back in her seat as if girding for the onslaught.

Duncan didn't disappoint her, even though he had planned to leave all of the talking to Reese. This was her day, her moment. This was her son. But curiosity had him asking, "I assume he's healthy, no drugs in his system at birth or fetal alcohol syndrome or, um, anything like that?"

Jenny frowned and divided a confused look between the pair of them. "Yes, he's healthy or at least there are no known medical issues. I thought I told Reese that when I called yesterday."

"You did," he recovered. "Sorry. I just…I just wanted to be sure."

"If you're looking for guarantees, Duncan, I can't give you those." Jenny's gaze was direct, probing. No doubt she was recalling from their counseling sessions that this was one of the big issues he'd had with the whole process.

"I know you can't."

"No one can predict what the future might hold—not for you, not for him—not for any of us," she stressed.

God, how he suddenly wished that somebody could. Six years of guessing had worn a hole in the lining of his stomach that no antacid could soothe.

He pasted on a polite smile. "No, of course not."

"We wouldn't have had any guarantees with a biological child, either," Reese said quietly.

Duncan knew that and yet so much here was uncharted, unknown. It doesn't matter, he reminded himself. Time to change the subject. "So, he's...he's nearly three months old."

"Yes, as I told Reese yesterday, he was born full term at four-forty in the morning." Jenny supplied the date and the details as she leaned forward to select a sandwich.

He glanced at his wife, who was tracing the image of baby's face with a shaky index finger as she listened. She still looked shell-shocked, but there was a softness to her features, a relaxed quality that he hadn't seen there in months...maybe even years.

Without looking up, she said, "I see here that he weighed six pounds, fifteen ounces at birth, but how big is he now?"

"Well, according to his foster mom, he's put on nearly five pounds."

"And the birth mom?" Reese did look up this time. "In my excitement yesterday, I forgot to ask. Has she signed off?" There was a slight edge to the otherwise casual inquiry and some of the tenseness returned to compress her lips.

Duncan knew why. In their education classes they'd been told that there was no set time limit for a biological mother to surrender her rights. Even if the baby went directly into foster care from the hospital, as this baby apparently had, she was under no obligation or pressure to sever her ties. Most did so within a couple of months of giving birth, eager to start healing emotionally and to get on with their lives. But Jenny had told them that she knew of a couple of worst-case scenarios where a baby—and the adoptive parents—had waited in excruciating limbo for several months before the deed was finally done.

"The father signed off the day the baby was born. The mom did so just after the first of the year."

Duncan felt his polite smile slip a notch. How was that for ironic? The baby Reese had been waiting for so desperately had been released for adoption before Duncan had packed up his bags and left their home.

If she found the situation ironic, she didn't let it show. "That means—"

"That means the twenty-eight-day waiting period for her to petition to have her rights restored ended Monday," Jenny interrupted with a grin. "I held off on calling you, even though she'd picked you and Duncan three weeks before going into labor. I have other clients that I'd feel comfortable notifying right away. In your case, given all of the heartache you two have gone through…" She motioned with one hand and her smile turned sympathetic. "It just seemed best to wait."

During those weeks the young woman could have changed her mind for any reason and made her petition. Now she had no legal claim to the infant. Duncan heard Reese let out a ragged sigh. Then, after a slight pause, she asked, "So, what is the mother like?"

For the next twenty minutes, Reese peppered their caseworker with questions about the birth parents—both of whom were college students. And the foster mom—an older woman who had taken in and cared for more than forty infants during the past twenty-four years.

Then Jenny asked a question of her own.

"Do you have a nursery set up? I know you said you'd taken down the crib after your last miscarriage."

Reese shook her head. "No. It's still down. It was just too hard to pass that room and look at it after…well, afterward."

Duncan felt his gut twist as memories reeled him back. He and Reese had gone together to her doctor appointment. They'd been happy and excited because they had decided to find out the baby's sex. When the ultrasound began their doctor was smiling, joking with them and asking if they'd picked out names. A few moments later, his expression had sobered.

There had been no mistaking the sympathy in his tone when he told them, "I'm sorry, Mr. and Mrs. Newcastle, but I can't find a heartbeat."

The doctor had sent Reese directly to the hospital, where, because she was in her second trimester, she'd had to go through the agony of labor even though the outcome had already been a given. Their baby, a girl, was dead. Just the day before, they'd put up the crib. That night, Duncan had gone home alone to disassemble it. Reese had begged him to. She didn't want to see it when she came home in the morning, she'd told him. He knew exactly how she felt.

Duncan had never cried in front of his wife. In fact, he'd never openly grieved the loss of either child, let alone the incremental loss of hope for biological offspring. But he'd done so when he carried the small mattress up to the attic. He'd stored it and the rest of the crib behind the boxes containing Christmas decorations and then he'd sat on the dusty floor for two hours, alternately cursing God and begging him for help.

The following day, when Duncan had picked Reese up from the hospital, she'd sobbed all the way home. He'd been dry-eyed and stoic. Insensitive, she'd later claimed. But one of them had needed to be strong.

"We'll bring the crib down from the attic,"

he told her now. He didn't realize he'd reached for her hand until he felt her fingers squeeze his. Oddly it sounded like a vow when he added, "We'll put it back together."

God, if only it were that easy to reassemble their deconstructed lives.

"That can be your homework for tonight," Jenny teased, breaking the somber moment. Her upbeat tone helped shorten the long shadow cast by grief when she added, "By this time next week I'd like to have the baby moved permanently into your home. Between now and then, you'll have an opportunity to see him, bond with him at the foster mom's and set up a proper nursery. How does that sound?"

"Like heaven," Reese replied in a breathless whisper.

Jenny turned her gaze to Duncan. "You've been pretty quiet for most of our conversation. What do you think?"

He cleared his throat and sat up straighter under her assessing stare. Beside him on the couch he felt Reese stiffen and her grip on his hand grew tighter as if she was worried about what he might divulge.

"It's a lot to process," he began.

"But in a good way," Reese inserted. Her laughter sounded forced and nervous.

Jenny's brows rose. "Duncan?"

He cleared his throat again. He was uncomfortable lying outright and so he evaded her question with, "I'm still having a hard time believing that the adoption is actually happening and so fast."

"Fast? It's taken forever." To mitigate her clipped tone Reese smiled, but even before she released his hand Duncan knew their one moment of harmony had ended.

She opened the file folder again and Duncan's gaze was drawn to the photograph inside. The baby seemed to stare back at him and his emotions churned, tumbling around inside his head like rocks inside a polishing machine.

"I guess I'm not sure what I'm feeling," he admitted at last. Interestingly that much was true.

Despite the overall vagueness of his response, Jenny seemed satisfied with it.

"It's okay, Duncan," she assured him. "You're entitled to that. It might not seem real for a while, especially during this interim period when you're just visiting with the baby for a few hours at a time at either the agency or the foster mom's home. Once your son is here, though, and you're getting up at two in the morning, it will sink in."

Your son. The simple words rocked him. They were wrong, inaccurate. They were an outright lie. Even so, hearing them did strange things to his heart.

"By the way," Jenny said. "What are you going to name him? I'll need to let the foster mom know so she can start calling the baby that, get him used to hearing it."

Reese nibbled her lower lip for a moment. "We haven't really decided," she began.

For some unfathomable reason, however, Duncan had. "Daniel," he said unequivocally. "His name is Daniel."

CHAPTER THREE

REESE and Duncan stood together, framed like a photograph in their home's entryway, and waved goodbye to Jenny. As soon as their caseworker's older model Chevy was out of view, though, Reese's smile disappeared and she wilted back a step. Duncan did the same on a heavy sigh and closed the door. They stood on opposite sides of the dimly lit foyer and studied one another for a long moment.

His name is Daniel.

Reese was still stunned over his answer to Jenny's question about what they planned to call the baby. Stunned and deeply moved.

Duncan wanted to name her child after Daniel Clairborne, the man who had been like a brother to him? His best friend's death had devastated him, coming so closely on the heels of Reese's second miscarriage. It was one of the few times she had known her husband to cry, and she'd needed to believe that with those harsh, broken sobs she'd heard coming from behind the locked bathroom door Duncan had also grieved the babies that had been lost. He certainly had never grieved for either unborn child in front of her.

Given the special meaning the name held, she'd assumed Duncan would want to save it for the biological heir he so desired. Yet there had been no hesitation, no wavering whatsoever. He'd sounded certain, resolute, almost as if in giving the name he was laying claim to the child.

That was crazy, she chided herself. Ridiculous. Only a foolish woman would try to make something of it. Only a foolish woman would look for hidden meanings and motives. I can't afford to be a foolish woman, Reese told herself as she watched him now.

"I think that went well," she said at last.

"Yes." Duncan nodded.

She studied her hands for a moment, played with the gold band that encircled the third finger on the left one. "You know, I really like Jenny. It's difficult to keep the truth from her."

She expected Duncan to agree, but he said, "I've been thinking about that. What 'truth' are we keeping from her, Reese? We're still married. That's not a lie." He pointed toward her hand. "You're still wearing your ring."

"It's not a ring," she murmured before she could think better of it.

Duncan's gaze sharpened. "No. It's not a ring."

It was a promise. That's what he'd told her when he'd slipped the gold band onto her finger all those years earlier.

This isn't a ring, Reese. It's a promise I'm making to you. I will love you till the day I die.

He hadn't kept his promise. Even so, he still had on the gold band she'd given him, Reese noticed now. Her promise. One she had kept— would keep always—even though doing so sometimes felt as though it was killing her.

"I see you're wearing yours, too," she said. Was it just a prop, put back on for Jenny's benefit?

"Why wouldn't I be?" he countered smoothly. "As I said, we're still married."

The words echoed in the foyer, oddly challenging. If she had been feeling braver she might have pressed him for an explanation, but she wasn't feeling brave right now. No, she was feeling confused and excited, hopeful and nervous and about a dozen other emotions that she couldn't name as the baby's face floated front and center in her mind.

She fidgeted with her hair, tugging it out of the ponytail and then gathering it all together again to secure it with the same rubber band. As she did so, she asked casually, "So, what do you think of him?"

"The baby?" His tone turned cautious.

"Uh-huh."

"Well, he's…he l-looks…" Duncan stuttered uncharacteristically as he stumbled around for words. Finally half of his mouth tugged up in a smile that did funny things to her heart. "God, he's a cute little guy, huh?"

"Beautiful," Reese corrected, but she smiled, too. Then she tilted her head to one side. "You seem surprised."

Duncan shrugged again and his expression turned guarded. "I guess I thought...I mean, I guess I was expecting..." He leaned back against the wall, pinched his eyes closed and shook his head ruefully. "Hell, Reese, the truth is I don't know what I was expecting."

His candor shocked her and so she decided it deserved to be returned. "Me, either," she admitted softly.

His lids flicked open and blue eyes stared at her intently for a moment. "Really?" More than intrigued, he sounded relieved.

"It's new territory for me, too, Duncan. I have no prior experience here, either."

He frowned. "But you've always seemed so confident that this was the right path. You've always sounded so sure when it came to adoption."

"What other choice have I had? Other than through surrogacy, which is an option neither one of us felt comfortable pursuing, this is the only way I can become a mother."

For once he didn't argue the point by bringing up the specialist in Chicago. "It doesn't seem real," was all he said.

"I know."

"Maybe it takes seeing more than a photograph for reality to sink in."

She didn't mention that their other babies had seemed real, their places in her and Duncan's hearts sealed long before they could even be glimpsed on an ultrasound.

"Maybe," she allowed.

"Well, this time tomorrow…" He left it at that.

"Yep, this time tomorrow I'll be holding him." Reese smiled and lifted her arms. She could almost feel the snug weight of a baby cradled there. Her throat grew tight.

Duncan pushed away from the wall and squared his shoulders. "Are you going to drive to the agency straight from work?"

She swallowed away the ache. "Actually, I'm taking the day off. Margaret is being wonderful about this," Reese said of the principal at the public school where she taught. "When I talked to her this morning, she immediately got to work on setting up subs for the next couple of weeks."

"Surely you're going to be out longer than that." He frowned.

"Yes. I'm thinking through the end of the marking period in June. That will leave me with the rest of the summer to look for a good day care and to prepare to go back for the following school year."

"You'll return to teaching in the fall?" His frown intensified until the space between his dark brows disappeared into a deep groove.

"I can't afford to take more time off than that."

She picked at one cuticle to avoid looking at him after she said it. Long ago, she and Duncan had decided that when a child came along Reese would stay home full-time for the first five years. But that was...before.

"No, I guess not," he replied after a long pause. "So, I'll pick you up here tomorrow?"

"Or we could just meet at the agency. Driving back to the house from your office is a little out of the way."

"I don't mind. Besides, I think we should arrive together."

Ah, yes, appearances. Even so, she hesitated a moment before finally nodding. "Okay." She smiled again. "Thanks. I would appreciate that."

He muttered something.

"Excuse me?"

"Nothing," he claimed, but she swore it had sounded like, "Great, more damned gratitude."

"Are you hungry?" She hitched a thumb over her shoulder in the general direction of the kitchen. "I can whip up something for dinner."

"Cucumber sandwiches?" Amusement lit his eyes briefly, banishing some of the awkwardness she was feeling.

"Hey, it's your mother's recipe," she reminded him.

"I know and enough said." His lips twitched and she couldn't help but chuckle softly in return.

"We could order Chinese."

"Nah. I had a big lunch. Besides, I'm not really feeling all that hungry right now."

"Me, either," she admitted. Then Reese wrapped her arms around her middle as nerves fluttered anew in her stomach. "God, Duncan, it's almost too good to be true. I don't know that I'll be able to sleep a wink tonight."

"Something tells me we should be sleeping while we have the chance," he replied wryly. In the low light of the foyer, he seemed to blush.

We, he'd said. They wouldn't be *we* for long. In reality, they weren't even *we* right now, Reese reminded herself. Yet it felt so good to have someone to talk to and confide her hopes and fears in at the moment. Earlier in their marriage, he'd been such a good sounding board. They'd talked openly, honestly about everything. They'd been so in tune that they could finish one another's sentences. With each failed fertility treatment cycle, each miscarriage, communication between them had become more strained and static-filled. Finally they'd both deemed it futile. She'd hated the silence. She loathed it no less now and so she kept talking.

"I still don't think I'll sleep. What if I wake up in the morning and it turns out this was all just a really good dream?"

"It's no dream, Reese."

Duncan stepped closer and reached out to run his knuckles over her cheek. Her breath hitched. Her heart stuttered. The unexpected contact caught her so off guard that it had her leaning in and yearning for more. She was a physical person, touching others often. An arm squeezed during conversation. A back patted. A cheek kissed in passing. It was the way she'd been raised. Duncan's upbringing had been just the opposite. Yet, in the early days of their marriage, he'd seemed to overcome his reserve when it came to physical displays beyond actual sex.

Hold me.

Reese nearly said the words out loud. Before they could be uttered, though, Duncan had stuffed both of his hands into the front pockets of his khakis and was walking away.

Just as well, she told herself. Just as well.

A few minutes later when Reese entered the den with the file folder in her hand, Duncan was seated at their computer on the distressed leather desk chair that she still felt they'd paid way too much for. But then Reese had always believed in hunting for bargains, whereas Duncan had rarely checked the price tag before making a purchase.

"We can afford it," he'd said often enough during their marriage. That was true, but Reese had been raised to believe one shouldn't spend money needlessly or recklessly. Since she would soon be returning to a single paycheck that was substantially less than Duncan's robust six-figure salary, she was glad she'd never forgotten how to be frugal.

Duncan glanced over from the computer screen. "I'm just finishing up. Need to get on the Internet?"

"Yes." She held up the folder. "I thought I'd scan the baby's photo and send it to friends and family. I know my parents are dying to see him."

"The cyberspace equivalent of a birth announcement?"

"Uh-huh."

"You could hold off until tomorrow, take a picture with our digital camera and then send a more recent shot to everyone," he suggested, leaning back in the chair.

"I'll probably do that, too, but I can't wait a whole twenty-four hours to share our—" She cleared her throat. "The good news."

Duncan nodded and held out a hand for the

picture. "I can do that for you," he offered, apparently remembering that she didn't have a clue how to operate their scanner.

"Thanks."

While he worked, Reese walked to the opposite side of the room. Bookshelves made of oak bracketed the large window that faced the front yard. A leather love seat sat between them and provided the perfect spot to curl up and bend the spine of a novel on those nights when she couldn't sleep. Tonight promised to be one of them.

The room was one of her favorites. It was the first one she and Duncan had remodeled after buying the house. They'd even done some of the work themselves, although he'd drawn the line at refinishing the wood floors. He'd never done a lick of what he called "manual labor" before meeting her, but he'd helped Reese paint the walls a rich terra-cotta and then he'd surprised her by having some of her artwork matted and framed. A trio of her oils hung next to a well-known artist's dreamy landscapes, which were valuable enough to require riders on their homeowner's insurance. Duncan had insured hers as well, as though some thief would bust in to take a Reese original.

She'd teased him about it at the time.

"You're just as good," he'd replied in all seriousness as he'd hung them.

Reese wasn't and she knew it. Indeed she had long ago accepted that her true talent lay in teaching rather than painting. She'd found joy and fulfillment in helping young people discover their gifts. Teaching, she believed, was an art form, too. Nonetheless, Duncan's blind support had touched her. Even now, as she ran her finger over the edge of one of the frames, she remembered his love-based conviction and felt a welling of emotion.

God, how had they let that get away?

"Photo's ready."

Back still to him, she nodded and hastily blinked away the tears. When she turned, no moisture remained as she smiled her thanks.

In little more than the time it took to attach the file, Reese had sent the photograph to every person in her e-mail address book.

"Check out our son!" the subject line read.

The "our" was for appearances, she told herself, and apparently Duncan agreed since he asked her to send the photograph to his friends and family members as well.

"They'll need to know," he said with a casual shrug as he leaned against the edge of the heavy desk.

He was so near that she could smell his cologne, that crisp, bold scent he'd worn for as long as she'd known him. She inhaled deeply, lost in memories.

"Reese?"

She realized she'd been staring. Angry with herself, her tone was a little sharp when she muttered, "Fine."

"Well, it's not like we can keep a child a secret for six months." He sounded slightly irritated.

"No. Of course not. We have other secrets to keep," she reminded him needlessly.

She thought of those secrets half an hour later when Duncan pulled on his wool coat and headed for the door.

Where are you going?

She didn't ask, just as she didn't inquire what time he planned to return. Nor did Duncan supply the answer to either of her unvoiced questions, even though suspicion

hung in the air between them as thick and ob-
scuring as a dense fog.

It was only five minutes past seven
o'clock, but it was already full dark outside.
The streetlights had winked on an hour ago
along with the lantern-shaped landscape
lights that followed the path from the porch
to the driveway. As Duncan backed the car
out onto the street, Reese stood at the
window in their living room, lowered the
blinds and tried to ignore the ache in her
chest.

Duncan arrived at his parents' house just in
time for after-dinner cocktails in the library. It
was a Newcastle tradition. His family was big
on traditions and he'd been taught not only to
respect them, but to see to their continuation.

He'd done his part, too. He'd gone to
Harvard and joined the same fraternity as a
legacy, making him the fourth generation of
Newcastle men to attend the Ivy League
school. He belonged to the elite social club
his great-great-grandfather, a Great Lakes
shipping magnate, had helped found. He'd
gone into banking like his father and uncle

and grandfather before him, even though other disciplines had called to him, architecture in particular.

Traditions lent stability. They were the thread that tied one generation to the next. That's what he'd been taught. That's what he'd always been told when he'd questioned some of his family's rigid ways.

In truth, he'd long suspected that some of those traditions were rooted in intolerance, indifference or outright fear of the unknown more so than any real allegiance to things past. Indeed even his parents' evening vodka martinis seemed less about spending time unwinding together after a hard day than discreetly dulling the senses enough to make a long evening spent in one another's company endurable.

God, he'd never wanted a marriage like theirs. One filled with cold silences, tempered emotions and measured looks. How was it that he'd wound up with exactly that?

As usual, his father was slouched in his leather easy chair near the fireplace, his craggy face half-hidden behind the newspaper, which was no doubt open to the stocks page. His mother was seated on a camel-back couch next to a curio cabinet where her collection of crystal figurines caught the overhead light and added the only bit of whimsy to the otherwise oppressively decorated room. The muted décor was another bow to tradition.

"Bold colors are faddish, dear," she'd told him upon seeing the terra-cotta walls of their den.

"Ah, this is an unexpected surprise." Louise set aside the magazine she'd been reading and smiled, but her words held a note of censure when she added, "You haven't been by in more than two weeks, Duncan."

Not since he'd moved out of his home. Staying away had seemed the wisest course of action to keep her from guessing the trouble in his marriage. His mother had never been particularly fond of Reese and he'd felt no need to validate her outspoken contention that he should have married someone more like himself. His parents were two of a kind, yet that certainly hadn't guaranteed compatibility and happiness.

"I've been busy," he lied. "Work."

He waved one hand dismissively and settled into a chair situated halfway between his parents. The middle ground. It was the position he'd staked out in childhood, but longevity had never made it more comfortable.

His father nodded in understanding as he folded the newspaper and laid it aside. Grayson Newcastle knew all about keeping long hours—whether at the office or at the club. What better way to ignore one's marital problems than to keep one's distance from his spouse?

Like father like son, Duncan thought now, for hadn't he done that during the past several months? Wasn't that exactly why Reese suspected him of having an affair?

Louise glanced toward the door. "Isn't Reese with you?" she asked politely. Not surprisingly, her expression registered not so much as a morsel of disappointment when Duncan told her that he was alone.

"I suppose she's busy with work, too." His mother's lips thinned.

Duncan exhaled slowly between his teeth. He felt unbearably tired all of a sudden. Just like with his parents, he always felt caught in the middle between his wife and mother, trying to explain one woman to the other.

"Would you like a drink, son?" His dad stood to refill his own glass from the pitcher of vodka martinis that had already been prepared.

God, yes! More than anything. And because it was true, Duncan shook his head. Alcohol wouldn't make his announcement any easier given his mother's outspoken views on adoption.

"Actually I can't stay long. I...I just stopped by to share some long-awaited good news."

Oddly the smile that accompanied his words wasn't forced in the least. In fact, it was uncomfortably genuine as his memory pulled up the image of tiny bunched fists and a pair of wide eyes.

Eyes shaped like Reese's.

His mother set aside her martini glass on the low table in front of her. Excitement had her uncrossing her legs and leaning forward. "Oh? Does it have anything to do with a baby?"

"As a matter of fact, it does."

The beginnings of a smile softened the

stern lines of her face. "Has Reese finally come to her senses and agreed to go to Chicago?"

Duncan shook his head. "We won't be going to Chicago." Disappointment welled, but its source was not readily clear, even when his mother sighed dramatically and shifted back in her seat.

"I'll never understand why she is so intractable on the matter. Further treatment might be available. Why not at least check into it?"

"She's had enough," Duncan said simply, and then he frowned.

Reese had told him that how many times? Like his mother, however, he'd pressed ahead in his quest for answers, for reasons, for cures. He'd been single-minded, determined. Wasn't that the same thing as being intractable?

His part in the whole matter had been limited to providing a sperm sample. Embarrassing, sure, but hardly on par with the seemingly endless rounds of shots, blood draws and laparoscopies that Reese had had to endure.

And then there were the miscarriages. He

felt the ache under his breastbone, pulsing in time with his heartbeat. It never quite went away.

"*She's* had enough," his mother was saying. Her riled tone chafed. "What about you? Doesn't she care what *you* want?"

That had always been his response, too. For the first time, it rang hollow.

"Louise, why don't you let Duncan share his news?" Grayson suggested diplomatically.

She huffed out an irritated breath and reached for her martini.

Duncan had brought the picture of the baby with him and he pulled it out of the breast pocket of his shirt now. The small face stared up at him, further tangling his already twisted emotions.

"The adoption agency called yesterday to tell us a birth mother has picked us. There's a baby…a boy. He's just a few months old."

He ran his index finger back and forth over the corner of the photo. The subtle snapping of the thick, glossy paper was the only noise in the room.

"Adoption?" his father said at last. His perplexed tone made it seem as if he'd never heard the word before even though Duncan and Reese had discussed the issue with his parents at length in the past.

"Yes, sir." Duncan cleared his throat and then forced out a laugh. "You know, it's amazing, but I swear the baby actually looks like Reese."

He turned the photograph face out, holding it first in his mother's direction and then in his father's. Only Grayson leaned forward for a better look. Neither one of them reached for it, though. His mother gave her martini a stir with the plastic stick on which a pair of plump olives was skewered.

"So, what's wrong with him?" she asked.

"There's nothing *wrong* with him."

"People don't give away perfect children, Duncan," she replied. She'd said the same thing before, at least a dozen times. Part of him had always agreed with her. Now, he wasn't so sure.

"What is a perfect child?" He directed the question at no one in particular as he tucked the photo back into his pocket. His hand lingered there for a moment and he didn't miss the fact that it was the pocket over his heart. "Can you tell me who has one of those?"

"You know what I mean, dear."

Did he?

She went on. "It's a different class of people that finds itself in the sort of situation that requires giving away offspring." The words were spoken sincerely and with an air of superiority. He recognized his own bigotry in them.

"And it's a different class of people that adopts."

He intended the comment to be snide, but his mother nodded in agreement. His father remained damningly silent. Duncan didn't know why he felt so let down. What did it matter? This was pretty much what he had expected their reactions to be. There were no surprises here.

"Well, I'd better be going," he said as he rose to his feet and smoothed down the front of his khakis. "Tomorrow is a big day. We'll be seeing the baby for the first time. I just wanted to drop by and give you the news in person."

"Can't you talk her out of this?" his mother asked.

"No."

Did he still want to? He wondered that as he recalled the awe on his wife's face that afternoon. And then he swallowed hard, remembering his own forbidden excitement. It was vicarious, he was sure. He felt it on Reese's behalf.

Even though his parents didn't ask him to, he said, "I'll call you tomorrow. Let you know how everything goes."

CHAPTER FOUR

REESE stood at the front window with her coat on, scarf knotted loosely and her purse slung over one shoulder, and waited for Duncan. He wasn't late, but she was anxious. No, she corrected herself, not anxious. She knew he would come and then they would be on their way. She was eager, which was something altogether different. Eagerness was a luxury she hadn't allowed herself to feel in years.

She was ready, more than ready, for this moment. She'd had nearly six years to prepare…and less than twenty-four hours.

Stuffed into her purse were the digital camera, battery fully charged, and a notebook filled with questions that she wanted to ask the foster mother. Draped over her arm was a small blanket that she had

quilted herself a year into their marriage—
long before it had become too painful to have
the kind of dreams each stitch represented.

She'd found the blanket tucked up in the
attic, in a box near the dust-coated crib. She'd
brought it down the night before and washed
it. Now, as she waited for Duncan to arrive, she
rubbed the soft fabric between her fingertips
and imagined that she was stroking her child.

A moment later, she spied his car turning
down their street and sighed in relief. Even
allowing for traffic, which would be light
this hour of the day anyway, they would have
plenty of time to make it across town for
their appointment.

Excitement thumped again and chased
away some of her disappointment from the
night before. Duncan had returned just
before ten and then disappeared into the
guest room before she'd had a chance to ask
him about setting up the crib. It was
supposed to be their "homework" and he'd
seemed so sincere when he'd promised that
he would help her put it back together. In
fact, for a brief moment she'd allowed
herself to believe he'd been talking about

more than the crib when he'd made that vow. But then he'd gone out.

How had he passed the evening? Reese had spent the better part of it gabbing into the telephone, spreading the joyous news to her family and best friend and trying to ignore the persistent undercurrent of despondency that threatened to submerge her good mood.

She'd called her parents first, of course. Reese smiled now and fiddled absently with the cord that lowered the blinds, recalling how she'd had to talk them out of getting on the next plane to Detroit. They were so eager to greet the baby, to hold him and welcome him in to the fold. He was the first grandchild. Reese's sister, Rochelle, was not due for another two months yet. And he was a miracle, or so her mother had declared over and over in her watery voice that had had Reese crying in return.

Reese had called her younger sister next, and felt warmed all over again by her enthusiasm. Rochelle, too, had wanted to come out from Boston to see the baby, but she would have to content herself with e-mailed photographs for now. Rochelle's blood pressure was up and her obstetrician had ruled out air travel for the remainder of her pregnancy.

"Maybe we can come out to see you after your baby is born. Daniel will be five months old by then." She'd sucked in a breath, letting it out on a sigh. "Can you believe our babies will be so close in age?"

"No, but I'm glad, even if you did have to go and beat me to the finish line," Rochelle had teased.

Reese had laughed in return, even though she'd known that the finish line was far from crossed. No, it waited in the distance, with a gauntlet to be run before victory could be claimed.

Finally Reese had called Sara Tucker. Sara was her best friend and the only person on the planet in whom Reese had confided her suspicions that Duncan was having an affair. She was also the only person who knew he had moved out and was now home, pretending everything was fine.

After squealing over the baby—she'd already downloaded the photograph and had been trying to get through on the busy telephone line for the better part of an hour—she'd asked pointedly, "So, how did it go with Duncan?"

"Good, actually. Very well."

"What did he think of the baby?"

"I think he was blown away," Reese had commented, recalling the look of wonder that had softened his features and drawn up his mouth. "But it doesn't change anything. He's out right now." The words had been said for her own benefit, a stern reminder to her naively hopeful heart.

"Do you know where he went?" Sara had asked. She'd never been convinced he was having an affair.

"No. I didn't ask and he didn't say. If I had to guess, though…"

"Don't guess, Reese. Try to give him the benefit of the doubt. He moved home."

"Only because I've promised to make a divorce easy for him afterward."

"Are you sure that's the only reason?"

God help her, but she didn't want it to be. "I can't talk about this now, okay?"

"Sure." Her friend had waited only a beat before asking, "So, when do you want to have a baby shower? You're going to need a lot of things."

The next twenty minutes had been taken up with determining a guest list and other party plans, but even in her excitement Reese had found herself wondering over Sara's assertion and listening for the rattle of keys in the door.

Now, she didn't wait for Duncan to undo with the lock. Unable to contain her excitement, she was at the door and pulling it open before he'd reached the porch.

"Hi," she said, slightly breathless as they faced one another across the threshold. A nervous grin unfurled. "I'm ready."

"So I see." He smiled in return, looking a little nervous himself. "I need to grab something. I left the car running if you want to get in. I'll just be a minute."

He was as good as his word, back before she even had a chance to buckle her seat belt.

"What's that?" she asked, pointing to the bag he stowed in the back.

"A new video camera. I bought it while I was out last night."

Mystery solved. Or was it? How long did

it take to purchase a video camera? He'd been gone almost three hours. Where else had he stopped?

She wanted to ask, but instead she said, "You bought a new video camera?"

"Yep. State of the art. You won't believe how small it is. I remembered that the old one didn't work right the last time we pulled it out to use it."

When had that been? Three Christmases ago? Four?

Memories stirred. With a snort of laughter she said, "That's because you dropped it in the pool."

"What pool?"

"The pool on the cruise ship. Our second anniversary."

"Oh. Yeah." His gaze cut to her briefly. "I remember now."

And so did Reese. He'd been sitting poolside with his feet dangling over the edge, filming her as she waded in breastbone deep water in her bikini. She'd made her way over to him, levering herself half out of the water so she could whisper a bawdy proposition in his ear. His grip on the camera had loosened, made slack by a healthy dose of lust. The next thing they knew, the camera had slipped and fallen right into the pool.

"We had a good time during that trip," he murmured now.

Was he recalling the way they'd hustled back to their cabin and hadn't come out until dinnertime? Reese shifted in her seat, and felt a flush creep up her cheeks. God help her, she was.

She cleared her throat and said noncommittally, "It's always nice to get away."

"Hmm. What made us decide to go on a cruise?"

"It was an anniversary gift from your parents. One with an ulterior motive. Your mother thought if I would just relax, then I'd get pregnant."

"We relaxed. A lot." His lips twitched and he shot her a look.

"We still didn't get pregnant."

"No. But the trying part was a lot of fun."

Left unsaid was that it had stopped being fun. It had stopped being spontaneous or even enjoyable. Infertility had seen to that. Reese had hoped moving on to adoption would return some of the spark and excitement, but by then the gulf between her and Duncan had been too wide to breach.

She decided to change the subject. "So, the camera you bought is state of the art? I suppose you let the salesman talk you in to buying an extended warranty." She made a tsking sound and kept her tone light.

His tone was light as well when he replied, "It didn't cost that much extra and we could have used a warranty on our last camera."

"Point taken," she agreed on a nod. "Buying a new one was on my list of things to do after Jenny called. I haven't had the time, though, so thanks. I brought the digital, but still pictures just aren't the same somehow."

"No. Snapshots miss a lot." He stopped the car at a traffic light and glanced over at her. "I figured you'd want to record every ooh and ah."

Half of his mouth crooked up in a grin and Reese smiled in return.

"That I do." Her expression sobered then. "Daniel is going to have questions someday. He's going to wonder why his birth parents didn't keep him. He's going to wonder why they made the choices they did. I'm glad we'll have today on film. I want him to be able to watch the video and know without a doubt how much he is wanted and loved and that they made this possible."

"He will."

Duncan sounded confident, almost as if he planned to be there. Reese didn't feel confident. In fact, she felt a fluttering of fresh nerves as she stared out the car window at the passing traffic.

"Remember the essay we each had to write as part of our home study?"

He snorted. "The one in which I had to give my reasons for wanting to be a dad?"

He'd resented that, she knew. And she didn't blame him. It was rather galling to have to put down on paper what no biological parent was ever asked to explain.

"I wrote that I wanted fingerprints on my windows and juice stains on my rugs and crayon artwork to display on my refrigerator. I didn't list all of the wonderful things I knew we could offer a baby financially or go on about what great parents I thought we would make," she said. "I just want a child to love."

"I know," he said quietly. "You're going to be a good mother."

"I hope so, but my reasons are so selfish."

"What do you mean? Why do you say that?"

"There is nothing altruistic or high-minded about my decision to adopt. I just want to be a mom. I don't care how that miracle comes about."

"Should there be more to it than that?" he asked.

"Some people think so. One of the teachers I work with told me how lucky this baby is. She commended me for opening my home and heart to a nonbiological child. She made it seem like I'm doing something noble. Like I'm *rescuing* this baby." She settled her head back against the rest and exhaled loudly. "God, Duncan, if anyone is being saved here, I think it's me."

"A lot of people have misconceptions about adoption," he replied on a shrug.

The comment had her head snapping sideways. He should know, Reese thought.

He'd harbored so many of them. But all she said was, "Yes. A lot."

"I told my parents last night."

She blinked in surprise. "About the baby?"

He nodded and another chunk of his evening out—perhaps all of it?—was accounted for. She didn't want to feel relieved, but she did. Relieved and incredibly curious.

"So, did you give them a, um, full accounting of the situation between us?"

"No. It's none of their business," he insisted again. Then, "Besides, I didn't want to complicate things. I figure the fewer people who know that we're…that we're having difficulties, the better."

That made sense she supposed. Wasn't that one of the reasons she'd chosen to keep her family in the dark as well? And even though she was pretty sure she knew, she asked, "So, what was their reaction to the baby? How did they take the news?"

His expression didn't change, but his gloved hands tightened on the steering wheel and brown leather protested as it was stretched taut over his knuckles.

"They took it about as well as you think."

She nodded, imagining the encounter. "Ah, that means your father said very little and your mother asked you to try to talk me out of it."

"Exactly." His laughter held no humor.

"I'm sorry, Duncan."

He nodded once. His voice was just above a whisper when he said, "Yeah, Reese, I'm sorry, too."

His reply could be taken a couple of ways. She decided not to try to figure out which one was intended as they drove the rest of the way in silence.

By the time they arrived at the agency the lining of Duncan's stomach was on fire and he seriously regretted eating the spicy takeout order he'd consumed for lunch while sitting at his desk. That was where he spent most lunch hours, as well as most evenings these days, and he had the area 'eateries' numbers programmed into his cell phone.

As soon as the car was parked, he reached into the glove box for the roll of antacids he kept there and thumbed off two.

"Everything okay?" Reese asked. "You're not heading for another ulcer or anything?"

It was small of him, but he appreciated the worry in her tone.

"Nah. I've just been eating takeout a little too often lately. All that spicy food doesn't agree with me." He popped the chalky tablets into his mouth and chewed.

"Takeout? Doesn't…" She left the thought unfinished, but from the way her cheeks flamed, he knew what she was thinking. *Doesn't Breanna cook?*

Back to that, he thought on a weary sigh. Well, let her wonder. Jaw clenched, he got out and retrieved the camera from the rear seat. The splash of slush under their feet was the only sound as he and Reese made their way across the parking lot.

They were a full fifteen minutes early, but Jenny didn't keep them waiting. She ushered them down a long corridor to a room that seemed more appropriate for discussing business mergers and acquisitions than for meeting a baby. Half a dozen mismatched chairs were lined up around a long table. On the far wall was a projection screen and an easel that showed a diagram of the adoption triad—birth parents, adoptive parents and baby. The three would always be linked, they'd learned in their education classes. Duncan swallowed.

"Sorry that we have to use the conference room," Jenny apologized. "The other two meeting rooms are in use for the next half hour and I figured you wouldn't want to wait."

"No." Reese rubbed her hands together eagerly. "No more waiting."

"Why don't you take off your coats? Can I get you something to drink? Coffee perhaps?"

"Nothing for me," Reese said as she shucked off her coat and scarf and deposited them on one of the chairs. When she turned, her smile brimmed with such hope and excitement that Duncan's breath hitched. He'd missed seeing that quirky, off-center smile. He'd missed watching the way happiness could make her dark eyes dance.

"Duncan?" Jenny asked. "Would you like something?"

"Yes," he said, his gaze still on Reese. Then he blinked, shook his head. "I mean, no. I'm fine."

Jenny checked her watch. "The foster mom should be here in just a moment."

"We're early," Duncan said.

"That's not surprising. Or all that unusual. I've had couples show up an entire hour early." Jenny winked. "It's a big day."

"The biggest," Reese agreed. She rested her palms against her stomach and sucked in a deep breath.

Duncan said nothing, but when the conference room door began to open a few minutes later, excitement bubbled up inside him, too. He battled it back, fought to deny its very existence. This was Reese's day. This was Reese's baby. Of course, he'd have to be made of stone not to be happy on her behalf. That was why his chest felt so tight. That was why it had become so difficult to breathe.

A woman of about sixty entered the room. She carried a portable car seat, over which a blanket was draped, probably to protect the baby from the brisk winter weather. It made the moment surreal, though, turning it into an unveiling of sorts. Duncan stepped closer to the table, pulled by some invisible force, and watched the foster mother peel back the cover.

And then he was there, the perfect baby

from the photograph, only he was bigger now. His face was fuller, with another chin added below the first one. He was close enough to touch and because Duncan wanted to, badly, he stuffed both of his hands into his pockets. The baby was asleep, but even with his eyes closed and his little mouth slack, something about him seemed familiar. Something about him tugged at Duncan's heart. Given the circumstances, it made him uncomfortable. As unobtrusively as possible, he fell back a step.

Reese, of course, moved closer.

"I can't believe how beautiful he is!" She covered her mouth with one hand, but delighted laughter escaped along with a hiccupping sob. "And just look at all that hair!" she exclaimed softly.

She reached out with a shaking hand to stroke the fine cap of brown on the baby's head. Daniel's rosebud mouth puckered and he made a faint sucking sound that had all of the women sighing and laughing. Duncan frowned, unprepared and unwilling to process the emotions charging through him.

"Duncan and Reese Newcastle, this is

Maggie Preston," Jenny said, belatedly introducing them to the foster mom.

"It's nice to meet you." Duncan shook the woman's hand, relieved to refocus his attention.

Reese pumped her hand next. "Yes, sorry to be rude and ignore you."

"It's okay. I'm used to taking a back seat," Maggie replied on a robust laugh that caused the baby to stir again. "In fact, I'd be a little nervous about handing over one of my babies to adoptive parents who were more interested in making small talk with me than getting that first peek at their child."

"You've done this a lot, I take it," Reese said. She was holding one of Daniel's small hands and Duncan found himself wondering if the baby's pale skin was as soft as it looked, as soft as he remembered Reese's to be.

"Yes. I haven't had a full night's sleep in nearly twenty years." But she grinned as she said it, apparently more than happy to have traded uninterrupted slumbering for the largely uncompensated rewards of fostering. "Daniel here makes baby number forty-six."

"Forty-six!" Reese exclaimed. "I can't imagine."

Words failed Duncan as well, but not for the reason that had Reese shaking her head in wonder. Hearing someone else call the child by the name they had given him caused Duncan's heart to tremble.

This isn't real, he reminded himself. At least not for me.

Maggie divided a look between the pair of them. "So, which one of you wants to hold him first?"

"Reese will," he said quickly and backed up another step. "I'll…I'll get the camera."

While Duncan pulled the video recorder from the bag, Reese felt the pressure build in her chest. Tears blurred her vision as Maggie lifted the baby out of the carrier and then placed him in her waiting arms. Until that moment, he'd been someone else's baby. Until Reese brought him to her shoulder, breathed in his sweet scent and felt that downy hair tickle her cheek, he hadn't been completely hers.

Now he was. Now he was.

She closed her eyes on the tears that had

turned the room blurry. Some of them leaked out anyway and spilled down her cheeks. During the past six years she had shed an ocean of tears. These ones were different. These ones were cleansing. They were healing. They were welcome.

"Hello, my little one," she whispered, laughing even as she cried. "Here you are at last."

She rocked on one foot and then the other, settling into a rhythm that was ages old and yet so new to her. Daniel wriggled in her arms, making little grunts and squeals as he came awake. Careful to support his neck, she lifted him from her shoulder and held him out in front of her so she could see his face. Bleary eyes blinked and then seemed to clear. He regarded her stoically as if taking her measure. Reese had already memorized his every feature.

"I know you," she murmured, awed by the powerful sense of connection and recognition she felt. "I would know you anywhere. You're my son."

More tears came, wetting her cheeks and washing away the old heartache. As she brought him back to her chest and hugged him against her heart, she looked up to find Duncan with the camera, recording the moment. Their gazes locked over the small display screen that was levered out to one side. She swore his eyes were moist.

What was he thinking?

"Can you believe it?" she asked, trying to interpret his partially obscured expression and failing.

Duncan didn't know what to say. No words seemed adequate, not that it mattered. He had been buried by an avalanche of emotions and rendered mute. The sheer joy and the boundless love on his wife's face as she finally held a child in her arms left him dazzled. They left him undone. He felt just as he had the first time he'd seen Reese. Immersed and in far over his head before he'd realized he'd even fallen.

And he felt envious, too, because her long-held dream was coming true even as his had stretched that much farther beyond his grasp.

"Let me take the camera for a bit," Jenny suggested. "You all should be in the shot."

He couldn't refuse. How would that look?

"Oh. Sure." He handed it over after offering a brief overview of operating instructions. Then he crossed to where Reese was and stood stiffly by her side. He felt like a movie extra even though he knew Jenny expected him to have a starring role.

"Come on, Duncan, put your arm around her," Jenny coached on a laugh. "That's better. Keep smiling. Now I'll zoom in close so that just the three of you fill the frame."

Just the three of us.

With his arm around Reese's shoulder and the baby snuggled in her arms, Duncan wanted what the picture represented. He wanted it so desperately that his throat ached, his eyes stung. He turned his head slightly and Reese's hair tickled his chin. Before he could think better of it, he shifted closer and dropped a light kiss on her temple.

"You look so happy right now," he whispered, giving her shoulder a squeeze that brought her closer to his chest.

Reese's eyes widened and then her damp cheeks crinkled with a smile. "I feel filled up inside where I used to feel so empty. Maybe that makes the difference."

"It does." He lifted a hand to her face and brushed away the streak of tears.

"Do you want to hold him?" she asked.

He didn't. And he did. His heart tripped. Before he could step away or change his mind, he allowed Reese to settle the baby in his arms. Daniel took the handoff in stride. He blinked and yawned, one eye crinkling closed briefly. Each expression was more endearing than the last.

"He's so small," Duncan said, feeling slightly panicked. The baby seemed to weigh nothing. He was fragile, vulnerable. He needs me, Duncan thought. No, not me. He needs a father. And he knew a surprising amount of regret that it wasn't going to be him.

"Actually he's grown a lot," Maggie said. "You should have seen him when I picked him up from the hospital nursery a couple days after he was born. My goodness, he was just a peanut then although he had no trouble getting his point across loud and clear at three in the morning. Most nights he sleeps a good six to eight hours now, by the way."

"I wish I could have been there when he

was born," Reese said. "I feel like I've missed so much."

Duncan watched the baby wrap one small hand around his index finger. What will I be missing? he wondered.

"I have pictures," Maggie was saying. "I try to take a lot of each baby so I can make up an album for the adoptive family to keep."

"That's a great idea and very thoughtful." Reese stroked the baby's cheek.

"I do it for me, too," Maggie admitted on a sigh. "I get double prints so I can look back and remember them."

"It must be hard to let them go."

"I just have them for a few months, but yes. Each one is special. It's so easy to fall in love with them and I do. Who can resist a baby?" Maggie smiled then. "You probably have some questions about his schedule."

"A lot, yes." Reese sat down next to her at the conference table and pulled out a notebook. While she scribbled down Maggie's answers to her questions about mixing formula and feeding and nap times, Duncan held the baby and felt apprehension skitter up his spine.

It's so easy to fall in love with them and I do. Who can resist a baby?

God help him, but he couldn't allow that to happen.

CHAPTER FIVE

"I DON'T want to leave him," Reese said as the visit wound down. After one last kiss, she reluctantly handed the baby back to Maggie, who buckled Daniel into the car carrier seat, covering him this time with the blanket Reese had lovingly stitched so long ago.

"I know, dear, but it won't be long and he'll be in your home for keeps," Maggie assured her with a sympathetic smile.

"Yes. Use this next week to tie up any loose ends," Jenny said. "Believe me, you won't be getting much done after the placement is complete." She turned to Duncan then. "How is the nursery coming along?"

He cleared his throat, his gaze veering to Reese. "It still needs some work."

"Okay, well, concentrate on that this evening then," Jenny said. "Get a good night sleep and we'll see you tomorrow afternoon. Does the same time work for you?"

Reese nodded and worked up a smile for their benefit, but Duncan saw some of the old hollowness return to her eyes and his stomach began to burn all over again.

In the car on the ride home, she was too quiet. He couldn't stand it any longer. Reaching over, he plucked one of her hands out of her lap and gave it a comforting squeeze. He planned to release it, but he held on, stroking her palm with his thumb. She didn't pull away. Duncan realized he'd expected her to. It made the contact all the sweeter.

"We need to put up the crib," he said. "And set up the changing table. Since we have a little time yet, maybe we could have the room painted or have a wallpaper border or something put up."

That suggestion perked her up a bit.

"The room could use a fresh coat of paint. Yellow would be nice and sunny."

"Too girly." He wrinkled his nose.

"Well, blue is a stereotype."

"Not to mention a plot by a patriarchal

society to brainwash children into assuming gender-specific roles as adults," he finished for her.

She laughed, as he'd hoped she would. "I believe I'm becoming predictable."

"You?" He flashed a wry grin. "Never."

They were still holding hands when they stopped at a home improvement store to pick up a couple of gallons of paint. It was a task that took far longer to complete than he'd expected because Reese couldn't decide between Butternut Squash and Sunny Day.

"Which one do you think?" she asked, holding out a pair of paint chips for his inspection.

They looked nearly identical to Duncan, but he scratched his chin thoughtfully before pointing to the first one.

"Sunny Day? Are you sure?" she asked. "I was leaning toward Butternut Squash."

"Actually you didn't let me finish," Duncan said. He pointed again, this time reciting "Eenie, meenie, miney, moe," as his finger alternated between the two paint chips.

"Very scientific," Reese managed to say amid laughter.

He chuckled as well, pleased by their easy banter—until she put two rollers and an assortment of paintbrushes into the cart he was pushing.

"Why do you need two rollers and all of those brushes?"

"It's a two-person job."

"Oh? So Sara's coming over to help you?"

"Nope." Her dark gaze danced with well-remembered humor. Just the sight buoyed his heart. "You are."

Duncan grimaced, because it was expected. In truth, the idea of spending the rest of the evening with Reese, even performing manual labor, was far too inviting.

"Maybe we could call someone, like a professional?" he suggested.

"What professional is going to come over to our house on such short notice and work half the night? We can do this. It's not like it's rocket science or anything," she teased.

"You said that about the brick pavers and when we refinished the wood floor in the kitchen."

"This will be easier than laying a walkway or operating a sander, believe me. A couple of hours, tops," she told him with a confident smile.

Four hours later they were still at it. The only break they'd taken was for Chinese food, which they'd had delivered to the house around eight o'clock. They'd eaten it with disposable wooden chopsticks right out of the little white cartons while they sat cross-legged on the tarp-covered floor. They hadn't talked much, not during the break, not during the work, but the silence was companionable rather than awkward.

It was just after ten when Reese said wearily, "It looks like the second coat will have to wait till morning. Lucky for you, you'll be at work."

Duncan poured the paint left over in the roller pan back into the can and tamped down its metal lid. Without looking up, he said, "Actually I took the rest of the week off."

"You did?"

"Yes." He glanced over when he added, "And the next week, too."

"You took off two weeks?"

Reese's tone indicated surprise, but was she glad?

"Uh-huh."

As he studied her expression, she pushed the hair away from her eyes with the back of her wrist, leaving a yellow streak across her forehead. Her cheeks and the bridge of her nose were speckled with yellow droplets that competed for space with her freckles. She hated those freckles. He'd always loved every one of them.

Duncan straightened and pulled a handkerchief from his back pocket. After wiping off his own hands, he offered it to her. "You've got some paint on your face." He indicated the locations with his index finger. Of course, Reese's blind efforts only succeeded in creating more smudges.

"Why did you do that?" she asked.

Duncan ignored the question. He stepped closer and took the handkerchief from her. "Let me," he said. Gently rubbing the square of yellow-splotched linen across her brow, he murmured, "You're a mess."

"It's latex-based. It'll wash off with soap and water." She shrugged after she said it, but he saw her swallow and her eyes were wide and watchful.

"Even a mess, you're still the most beautiful woman I've ever seen."

She snorted out a laugh. "I'm not beautiful." Then she ducked her head, studied her paint-covered hands.

They'd had this conversation before, but it still surprised him. For someone who was so confident in so many other ways, Reese had never been secure in her unconventional looks. No, that wasn't quite right. She'd just never understood why her unconventional looks appealed to Duncan. He couldn't say, either. He just knew that put altogether her somewhat quirky features did. They always had. And from the way his pulse hitched now, he figured they always would.

He traced a finger lightly along her jaw before using it to raise her chin. "You're beautiful to me."

He watched the pulse beating at the base of her throat and memories beckoned. He recalled what her soft skin tasted like, what it felt like beneath his hands. Without planning to, he leaned down and settled his mouth over hers. The contact was fleeting, but sweet. It reminded him of the first time they'd kissed all those years earlier when they'd met at a party through his friend. She'd been new to town, having just taken a teaching post in the school district where Daniel Clairborne's mother worked as superintendent. After their lips had parted, Reese had laughed.

"You call that a kiss?" she'd had the audacity to ask, shattering his ego. But then she'd flashed Duncan a flirty, off-center smile and stepped forward. "Let me show you how it's done back in Boston."

She'd brought her lips to his and Duncan had been lost. They were engaged six months later and married less than a year after their first date. His mother had warned him repeatedly that he was making a huge mistake.

"She's not really our kind, Duncan," Louise Newcastle had insisted rather vocally.

His mother was right. Reese wasn't like them. She was a gust of fresh air blowing through a musty room, rustling curtains, sending loose papers swirling, turning the pages of opened books. Duncan had delighted in the disarray she'd brought to his overly ordered life. In turn, Reese had enjoyed some of the structure he'd provided. They'd complemented one another so perfectly…until infertility.

God knew, he regretted a lot of things from the past several years. But even knowing how his relationship with Reese had turned out, he found he couldn't regret their marriage.

Reese wasn't laughing now. She was watching him with heavily lashed dark eyes that held just enough interest to give him courage. So, he took the initiative and leaned forward again. This time the kiss wasn't brief. It was infused with heat, fueled by pent-up need. He pulled her to him, bringing their bodies flush. His hard angles melted into her soft curves. A perfect fit. God, it had been so long. Too long.

He groaned when he felt her slender arms wrap around him. Her fingernails raked provocatively down his spine and he was wondering if they should bother trying to make it to the bedroom or if the drop-cloth-covered floor would do when she stopped and pulled away.

Duncan swallowed an oath. He found a

modicum of consolation in the fact that she appeared to be just as shaken as he felt. Her breathing was labored, her face flushed. The hand that she raised to her mouth wasn't quite steady.

"Wh-why did you do that?" Reese asked.

He had no answer for her. At least not one he was willing to share. If he told Reese he still loved her, she wouldn't believe him. She didn't trust him. And Duncan didn't trust her. Not with his heart. So, he decided to respond to her earlier question instead.

"Taking a couple weeks off from work seemed like the kind of thing a new dad would do, especially since I have several weeks of vacation time coming."

"Oh. So, it's just for the sake of appearances."

Of course that would be the conclusion she'd reach. He shrugged and turned away to gather up the paintbrushes as the heaviness returned to his heart.

"Why else?"

"And the kiss? Why did you kiss me?"

He straightened and faced her, lobbing the question back. "Why did you kiss me?"

"I...I..." Her face tinted pink and she couldn't hold his gaze.

"Yeah, Reese. That was my reason, too."

"Well, it's not going to happen again. Sex isn't part of our deal."

"Sex? You call that sex? I know it's been a while for both of us, but I thought that was just a kiss." He managed a casual shrug, even though he still felt wound up tight enough to explode.

Reese's cheeks flamed red now. "You know what I mean. It's not why I asked you to move back in. We're no longer a couple, Duncan."

"Right. We just need to pass for one."

She nodded slowly. "For a short time, yes."

"Just like, for a short time, I need to pass for a dad." He wasn't quite successful in keeping the bitterness from his tone. It leaked in, every bit as corrosive as battery acid.

Reese didn't say anything. They stared at one another for a long moment before Duncan ended their emotional stalemate by walking away. He left her to clean up the mess by herself. He wasn't in the mood to be helpful. In fact, it was being helpful that had gotten him into his current predicament.

In the guest bathroom, he showered, letting the spray turn as chilly as his mood. But long after he'd heard Reese retire to the bedroom they once shared, Duncan lay awake on the lumpy mattress, unable to forget that kiss and unable to banish the memory of what it had felt like to hold that baby in his arms.

Both things made him ache, yearn.

When he finally fell asleep, he dreamed of making love to his wife while their son babbled and cooed in a sun-filled nursery. Was that baby Daniel? He never got a close enough look in his dream to be sure. Oddly enough, though, the baby's identity hadn't seemed to matter.

When Duncan awoke, his cheeks were wet.

Three days had passed since their initial visit with Daniel in the adoption agency's austere conference room. Duncan and Reese had seen the baby two more times. Each visit made Duncan more uncomfortable than the last. That initial bubble of excitement he'd experienced when holding Daniel just kept growing, and the bigger it got, the more worried Duncan became about how he was going to feel when it finally burst.

The first two meetings had been at the agency, but the third was at the foster mother's house. Maggie had generously opened her modest St. Clair Shores bungalow to them. This visit lasted longer, giving Reese a chance to change and feed the baby and then rock him to sleep in the comfy glider that dominated one corner of Maggie's small nursery. Duncan manned the camera and declined all offers to hold him.

The weekend was approaching. More visits were planned for Saturday and Monday at Maggie's house. Everyone had agreed Tuesday would be the big day. On Tuesday, Reese, Daniel and Duncan would sleep together under one roof as a family.

Sort of.

The paint in the nursery was dry. Reese had finished the job by herself. She'd worked all night after their argument, and then she'd slept for the better part of the next day. Despite living together, they managed to barely see one another. Duncan couldn't help but feel she was avoiding him. That suited him just fine. It kept him from allowing his thoughts to stray where they had no business.

He was on his third trip down from the attic with the last piece of the disassembled crib when he heard the telephone ring. He didn't bother calling for Reese to answer it. Just a few minutes earlier she'd left to go shopping. He decided to let the machine pick up the call rather than to risk bodily injury trying to hurry down the narrow stairs while clutching the heavy oak headboard.

As he reached the bottom, he heard a beep from the machine in the den followed by a woman's voice.

"Hey, Reese. It's Sara. I hope you haven't left yet because I have some bad news. It turns out I can't make it this afternoon. Something came up at work and I'm not really in a position to say no since I'm in line for that promotion. I was thinking we could reschedule for tonight or tomorrow. Call me back at my office, okay?" There was a pause and then Sara added, "Just in case you have left already, I'll try your cell. Talk to you soon."

Reese had mentioned that she and Sara were going to All Things Baby, a big local retailer, to register for gifts for the upcoming shower. Duncan had felt oddly left out, which was ridiculous. What did he need to go along for? It's not like Jenny would be there to see them picking out a stroller and fussing over outfits. And if not for Jenny's benefit, then why would he go? Since that kiss, they'd been careful to steer clear of one another in the house.

"I never liked shopping anyway," he grumbled aloud now.

Except with Reese. She could turn even a mundane trip to the grocery store into an adventure. Even picking out paint had been amusing, fun.

A cell phone trilled the opening notes of the *William Tell Overture*, interrupting his thoughts. It was Reese's phone. His had an old-fashioned ring. Boring, according to his wife. But a far cry more dignified to his way of thinking. She must have left her cell on the charger, which meant her friend had no way to reach her.

He rubbed the back of his neck, tugged at the ends of his hair. She could shop by herself, of course. She didn't need anyone's help to pick out all those little necessities and extras. Having made that determination, Duncan nonetheless retrieved his wallet from the guest bedroom, grabbed his car keys and coat and headed out the door. He couldn't let her do this alone. He knew what an emotional moment it was likely to be.

Reese stood just inside the automatic sliding doors of the vast baby specialty store, breathing through her mouth and waiting for her nerves to settle. There had been a time when just the sight of bibs and booties could make her cry. When shopping for a friend's baby shower was bittersweet and all but unbearable.

Not today.

Oddly enough, though, she felt like a fraud. As if she still didn't have the right to the coveted title of mother. She shook off the thought and checked her watch for the fifth time. Sara hadn't arrived yet. It wasn't like her friend to be late.

A young woman clad in a T-shirt bearing the store's logo approached. Reese guessed her to be about twenty years old. Her name tag said Brandi.

"Hi. Can I help you? You look a little lost."

"No, I…I belong here."

Brandi's eyebrows tugged together briefly and Reese wanted to kick herself for the defensive-sounding reply.

"Are you here to buy a gift?" Brandi tried again.

"Actually I'm waiting for someone. A friend of mine. We were supposed to meet here at three o'clock to register for a baby shower."

"Oh, when is your friend due?" Brandi inquired.

Reese felt heat rising in her face. "The shower is…the shower is for me."

She had unfastened her winter coat while she waited for Sara to arrive and Brandi's gaze now dipped discreetly to her slim waist. "When are you due?"

Reese resisted the urge to pull her coat

closed. "I'm…I'm not having a baby." She hesitated a moment before adding, "I'm adopting one."

Brandi grinned. "Oh, how cool. Are you going to Russia or China or someplace exotic to get it?"

"No. The baby is American. It's a domestic adoption."

Brandi nodded. "Cool," she said again. "I always thought I'd like to adopt a child someday, you know, maybe after having a couple kids of my own."

Reese managed to keep a smile plastered on her face. She'd heard this before and knew most people didn't realize the amount of time, money, patience and resolve the process involved. Nor the amount of heartache that often came beforehand.

"Good for you," was all she said.

"And good for you. Wow! You must be so excited."

"Yes, I am." The smile Reese gave the young woman this time was genuine.

"Do you know if it's a boy or a girl?"

"A boy. He's three months old and he's coming home on Tuesday." Just saying the words out loud made her heart flutter, her pulse trip.

Brandi motioned toward the customer service desk. "Well, when your friend gets here, come and see me. I'll get you set up with everything you need to register for your shower."

"Thanks."

When Reese turned back to look out the glass doors, she blinked in surprise. Duncan was striding across the parking lot with his hands tucked deep into the pockets of his leather coat. The wind ruffled his dark hair and turned his lean cheeks ruddy. Her heart knocked out an extra beat just at the sight of him before she could remind herself she was being foolish.

The doors parted and he stepped inside on a gust of frigid air.

"Hi," he said, pushing his hair back from his forehead.

"Hi. What are you doing here?"

"Sara called and left a message saying she can't make it this afternoon. Something came up at work. She said she'd try to reach you on your cell."

"But I forgot to bring it with me." Reese pursed her lips.

"I know."

"Oh. And you came all the way down here to tell me." She smiled. "That was really nice. Thanks."

"It's no big deal." He shrugged off her thanks, seeming oddly irritated by it. "Sara said she could go tonight or tomorrow if you wanted to reschedule."

"Okay." She began to rebutton her coat.

"Or, I thought maybe I could help."

Her hands stilled and she glanced up sharply. "You want to help me register for the baby shower?"

He lifted his shoulders. "I just thought… Forget it."

"No. I'm sorry. You just caught me off guard."

He seemed to be doing that a lot lately with little touches, thoughtful gestures…that damned kiss. God, she'd been burning ever since. And she'd been haunted by the comment he'd made. *You call that sex? I know it's been a while for both of us, but I thought that was just a kiss.*

A while for *both* of them?

He was watching her now, looking…self-conscious?

"You'd probably rather do this kind of thing with Sara anyway."

"No. I mean, we're here. Why don't we at least get the ball rolling? The shower isn't for nearly a month. So, we'll…um, the baby will need some things before then: Sleepers, bottles, diapers, linens for the crib. I planned to pick up some of that while I'm here today."

"Okay."

Brandi set them up with a little gizmo that scanned the bar codes of items they wanted and recorded them for the registry. It was simply a matter of walking up and down the aisles of the vast store and making selections.

They also had a cart so that they could pick up necessities along the way. Duncan was quiet for the first few aisles, not offering much of an opinion as Reese oohed and ahhed over everything from bath toys and burp rags to sippy cups and pacifiers. But then they came to the toy section and his eyes lit up like twin blue gemstones.

"He's got to have this," he said, pointing to an adjustable plastic basketball hoop.

The packaging of the box it came in showed a picture of an adorable toddler dunking a small orange ball. One was set up for display. Duncan picked up the ball and dropped it through the hoop. A cheerful buzzer sounded.

"You do realize that it will be a while before Daniel can use it?" Reese said, tucking away her grin. Her husband hardly looked like a stodgy bank president right now.

"Sure." He shrugged. "But it will be a while before he can use the potty chair. That didn't stop you from putting one on the list."

It wasn't quite the same, but Reese nodded anyway. She was too touched by the enthusiasm in his tone to argue or to point out that he wouldn't be there when Daniel starting walking. "Okay."

They continued down the aisle with Duncan leading the way. She was pushing the cart now and he held the electronic scanner, wielding it like a sword and taking no prisoners. In short order he had registered for an assortment of toys, with Reese adding in the educational ones she preferred.

"Hey, check this out." He picked up a small baseball mitt and filled the leather pocket with his balled fist. "I always thought it would be fun to teach my son to play catch. My dad never had time to do it, not that he cared much for baseball anyway." His expression turned nostalgic and just a touch sad. "I plan to make time for my son."

"Oh, Duncan," Reese murmured, not sure of the origin of the tears stinging her eyes.

He glanced up and his face reddened. "You know, someday. When I'm really a dad."

CHAPTER SIX

DESPITE the closed blind at the window, the nursery glowed yellow. It was a sunny day outside, even if it was bitterly cold. They would need a room-darkening shade, Reese thought, adding it to her growing mental list. She also was toying with the idea of painting a mural on the wall behind the rocking chair. It looked too bare. Maybe she'd sketch a scene from *Jack and the Beanstalk* or *The Frog Prince.*

Those things could wait, though. Nothing was more pressing at the moment than watching the rhythmic rise and fall of Daniel's small chest as he napped. He was home, sleeping in the very crib that for too long had held only heartache. Reese still couldn't believe he was here. She still couldn't believe he was hers.

With each breath he took, her heart swelled. She'd never known love like this. It was so boundless and consuming that it filled up almost every empty space inside her. She felt a kind of completion and a contentedness that left her awed and a little unnerved, because it still could all be taken away. That knowledge tempered her happiness. As did the fact that Duncan wasn't really part of it.

She needed to remember that.

When Jenny and Maggie were around Duncan was involved and attentive, manning the camera, playing the gracious host. He said all the right things, went through the proper motions of an eager and devoted new dad. Indeed he did so with such verve and finesse that at times he almost had Reese fooled. But then the moment the two of them were alone again, he distanced himself—literally and figuratively—from Reese and the baby.

Today, Daniel's first day in their home, was no exception. Jenny and Maggie had departed nearly three hours ago and since then Duncan had been in the den with the door closed, supposedly returning e-mails and checking on things at work, even though he was on vacation. As the bank's president, of course, it wasn't unusual for Duncan to take calls or teleconference even when he was out of the office. Still, his excuse on this day rang hollow.

And it served as a reminder that he had another life he was eager to start, one that didn't include an infertile wife or an adopted baby. Between now and their court date in six months, it wouldn't do to get used to having him around, much less to rely on him. Reese would soon start a new life, too, that of a single mother, which meant she needed to learn how to handle parenting on her own. She had to be able to shoulder all of the responsibility for Daniel's care, because in just a matter of months Duncan wouldn't be there.

"I'll love you enough for two parents," she whispered to the sleeping baby.

She made the vow and she meant it, but it caused her heart to ache a little as she wondered if someday Daniel would feel cheated to have only one parent instead of the traditional two, especially since he was a boy and would be without a father. The possibility of someday remarrying seemed remote to Reese. Who, after all, could she ever love as much as she had loved Duncan? As much as she still loved him.

Unbidden came the memory of him holding the baseball mitt in the store and smiling as he spoke of someday playing catch with his son. For a brief moment she had sworn that Duncan was as excited about the baby as she was. She'd almost believed that Daniel's parentage had ceased to matter to him. She'd almost believed that he'd finally gotten beyond the stumbling block of biology. But, of course, he hadn't.

"I guess I'll have to learn how to field a grounder and steal bases," Reese murmured.

"That can wait a little while." There was a smile in Duncan's voice, as well as one on his face when Reese turned to find him in the open doorway.

"Just thinking out loud," she murmured with an embarrassed shrug.

Duncan said nothing for a moment, then, "So, when did he go down?"

"About fifteen minutes ago. He dropped off while I was feeding him."

"That's a surprise." Duncan chuckled softly. "For a little guy, he sure likes to eat."

And Daniel did. He ate noisily, greedily, attacking the nipple on the bottle of formula as if he'd been deprived of sustenance for days rather than mere hours. She hadn't realized, though, that Duncan was paying such close attention.

"Well, he had pretty much finished off the seven ounces before his eyes shut for good."

"Figures." He laughed again. Then his gaze slid to the crib. "So what now?"

"Well, according to Maggie, he should be asleep for a couple of hours and then he'll be up for a couple more before going down again for the better part of the night."

"Hmm." Duncan's eyes narrowed. "That sounds a little too simple."

"Yes, it does." She shared his skepticism, even though she hoped they would be proved wrong.

"I guess we'll see."

"Uh-huh."

Duncan leaned against the doorjamb. Reese could tell something was on his mind even though his pose was relaxed and his expression nonchalant. After a moment, he said, "I called my folks."

"Oh?"

"I wanted to let them know the baby was here."

Reese had called her parents as well. She didn't doubt the Newcastles' reaction had been the polar opposite of the exuberance Maureen and Wally Deerfield had been unable to contain during their conversation. If her family lived nearby, Reese knew they would be in her home right now offering their congratulations and lending their support.

"So, what did they say?"

"They'd like to come by and see him."

Reese snorted. "Look him over, you mean."

His jaw tightened, but he nodded.

"When? Please tell me not tonight."

She knew she sounded rude, but just about the last thing she wanted to do on Daniel's first evening in their home was suffer through a visit with Duncan's mother, who was sure to find fault with everything from the way the nursery was decorated to how Reese was dressed. As for the baby, well, just let the older woman point out a single flaw. One negative word and she would be shown the door.

"No. Tomorrow. I told them I thought tonight, being his first night here and all, should be just..." He cleared his throat. "Us."

The word hung in the air between them, sounding like a challenge, sounding like a promise.

Reese smiled weakly, nipped by guilt and a softer emotion that was even more disconcerting.

"Actually I invited Sara over. She should be here in about an hour. She has a gift for the baby and, of course, she's dying to see him and hold him."

"Oh."

"Sorry."

"No, that's okay." He levered away from the jamb and waved a hand. "It was really just an excuse to get out of seeing my parents today. I'm not in the mood to put on another big show for anyone."

Duncan knew Sara was privy to their marital problems as well as the conditions under which he had returned home. He wouldn't need to act liked a proud new papa around her. Still, for some reason his answer disappointed Reese.

"Is it…that hard?" she asked quietly.

"Excuse me?"

"Pretending to want him. Pretending to love him."

Her gaze strayed to the crib, to the baby slumbering peacefully there. Daniel was so beautiful, so utterly perfect. Just looking at him took her breath away. How was it possible for Duncan to look at him and feel nothing?

"Reese."

When she glanced back at her husband, his eyes were pinched shut and he was shaking his head. He was…what? Angry? Offended? Hurt? Sad? God, she couldn't seem to read his moods any more.

"I'm sorry to be so blunt. I guess I just don't understand how—"

"It's not hard, okay? Is that what you want to hear? It's not hard."

She definitely detected anger then. And something else…the mere possibility of which had her swallowing.

"Duncan," she began, but before she could even form a clear thought, he had turned and was walking away.

The first night seemed to be going according to the schedule Maggie had laid out. Daniel woke after a two-hour nap and was up for a few hours, gurgling and waving his little arms and legs adorably for Sara as she and Reese sat on the edges of a blanket they'd spread out on the floor in the nursery. Then, after being fed, burped and changed, he dropped off to sleep again just after nine o'clock.

Duncan had busied himself elsewhere the entire time, offering only a polite greeting to Sara when she first arrived. But he hadn't gone out at least. Reese found comfort in that fact, even though she knew he'd made several phone calls. Had one of them been to Breanna? He hadn't seen her in days.

Could she be wrong about the two of them? He'd claimed she was off base from the start. No, she chided her hopeful heart, recalling his late nights at work and the aloofness when he was home. Just before

Christmas he'd stopped protesting his innocence and instead had started sleeping in the guest room. Of course, even when they had shared the same bed, nothing had been going on. They'd slept back to back, taking care not to touch one another.

After Sara left, Reese tidied the kitchen and straightened up the living room, plumping the pillows on the sofa and dusting the tabletops. She hadn't bothered with this before Sara's arrival, knowing her friend wouldn't find fault. Duncan's parents, however, were another matter. When they came by the following evening, Reese knew they would expect to find hors d'oeuvres and drinks waiting for them in an immaculate house.

The Newcastles had a staffed kitchen and a live-in housekeeper, which Reese supposed made sense given the vastness of their Lakeshore Drive estate. Well, she wasn't as fastidious or neurotic as Louise, and Reese's house was small enough that she could manage to keep its rooms reasonably tidy all by herself, although Duncan had been known to wield a vacuum and mop. Reese had had to show him how, of course. His mother was appalled.

Glancing around the living room, she smiled. She loved this house. It had so much character and charm. It also held a surprising number of good memories, she realized. As she ran the dust cloth over the surface of the coffee table, she recalled how Duncan had carried her over the threshold. The gesture had been sweet, chivalrous and utterly romantic— right up until the moment her head had thumped against the doorjamb. She grinned at the recollection. He'd felt so horrible.

"Kiss it and maybe I'll feel better," she'd coaxed suggestively.

After closing the door, Duncan had kissed much more than her bruised temple. He'd gone on to soothe a different kind of ache right there on the foyer's floor. Neither one of them had minded the hard surface.

Reese exhaled sharply and began to polish the table with a little more gusto, but for some reason the memories just kept coming, one more detailed than the last. How could she have forgotten that she and Duncan had made love in practically every room in the house?

Of course, at the start of their marriage,

lovemaking had been spontaneous, adventurous and immensely satisfying. Sometimes it had been over quickly, leaving them both scorched but smiling amid a tangle of clothes on whatever flat surface had been handy. Other times the pace had been more leisurely. There had been no hurried race to the finish, but a languid certainty that fulfillment would be coming and patience would make it all the better.

"Mmm," she murmured, closing her eyes.

She was fanning her face when Duncan walked into the room.

"Are you okay?" he asked.

Her eyes snapped open and she felt her flushed face became all the more heated. "I'm f-fine. Just doing a little housework."

He glanced around. "The place looks nice enough. Don't knock yourself out for my mother."

Reese moved the lamp back into place and adjusted the selection of art books on one of the end tables. She couldn't bring herself to look at him just yet.

"You know how she is."

"Yes, and so do you."

Indeed Reese did. The woman was picky, domineering and impossible to please. Those were some of Louise's better qualities.

"Well, the room needed to be dusted anyway." Reese shrugged, not liking in the least the fact that after seven years, she was still trying to gain the older woman's approval.

"We can afford to hire help."

He'd made this suggestion before, telling her that weekly maid service would ease some of the burden off both of them. He hadn't liked mop duty, but Reese figured it was good for him, made him understand and appreciate the little people who came into his bank seeking loans or cashing their modest paychecks.

"No. I prefer keeping my house myself."

"But now that the baby is here—"

"I won't be able to afford it, Duncan. My salary won't allow for it," she said flatly.

His tone was somewhat gruff when he said, "Well, don't work so hard."

"I'm not."

"Your face is flushed from exertion."

Oh, she was flushed all right, but the cause was something a whole lot more complicated than housework.

He stepped close enough so that he could touch her cheek. The light stroke of his fingertips unwittingly ratcheted up her body's already heated temperature. "It's been a crazy week with all of the changes and running around. Why don't you take it easy? Why don't you try to relax?"

"Relax," she repeated. That was an impossibility right now with him standing so close. His lightest touch had every muscle, every molecule in her body snapped to attention.

"Yeah." He grasped her shoulders with the same competent hands that had once known where to find every sensitive spot on her body. Massaging gently at first and then with a little more intensity, he said, "God, you're so tense, so tight."

His hands stilled then. His gaze lowered to her mouth. She knew that look. He was going to kiss her again. Part of her wanted him to. Part of her wanted him to do much more. She cleared her throat, stepped far enough back that he was forced to drop his hands.

"It's getting late, Duncan. I'd...I'd better finish up in here."

He sighed, shook his head. "Sure. I'll let you get back to what's important."

When Reese fell into bed an hour later, she was exhausted and eager for sleep, but two hours went by and she was still lying on her back, staring wide-eyed at the ceiling and feeling restless. In addition to wondering rather inappropriately if Duncan still preferred to sleep in only a pair of boxer shorts, she was fixated on the grunts and rustling sounds coming from the monitor. She'd had no idea that babies were such noisy sleepers.

It was a Catch-22, of course. Because when more than a few minutes of silence ensued, she got up to check on Daniel, ridiculously worried that he had succumbed to Sudden Infant Death Syndrome.

She was holding her hand near his face, relieved to feel the warm puffs of his breath on her fingers, when Duncan whispered from the doorway, "Everything okay?"

In the dim light she noticed his hair was tussled, as if he'd raked a hand through it more than a few times. He was shirtless and clad only in boxers. Her earlier question was answered. She'd seen him this way countless times during their marriage, but right now the mere sight of those long, nicely muscled legs and that taut abdomen did outrageous things to her pulse. She blamed several months of abstinence for her response, but it was more than that. It occurred to her then that even though their conversations weren't always completely pleasant, she and Duncan had talked more in the past week than they had in the past several months. Maybe there was hope that at least their friendship could be saved.

"Everything's fine," she whispered. "I just can't sleep."

When she joined him in the hall, Reese was determined to maintain eye contact. Friendship.

"Me, either."

Duncan didn't maintain eye contact. His gaze dipped and lingered on the snug-fitting pajama top she wore. She didn't have overly large breasts, but they were incredibly sensitive to the touch. His touch. He'd always told her they were one of his favorite features. His Adam's apple bobbed now and she swore she heard him issue a soft groan. Reese crossed her arms over her chest, telling herself she was embarrassed when in fact what she felt was…turned on.

"I—I had no idea how much n-noise babies make when they sleep," she stammered. "But then, of course, the minute he's quiet I start to worry. I've been in three times already to check on his breathing."

"I know."

"You know?"

"I've heard you."

"Oh." She felt like an idiot. "God, I'm such a rookie at this."

He chuckled softly. "Yeah, but I'm pretty sure all new parents must go through this."

"It's a lot of responsibility, taking care of an infant."

"An awesome amount," he agreed.

She motioned down the hallway to her bedroom door. "Well, I should try to get some sleep. If Daniel stays true to the schedule Maggie mapped out, he'll be up in a few hours wanting a bottle and needing a diaper change."

"I should go back to bed, too," Duncan said.

Neither of them moved, though. In the

room behind them, the baby grunted and then made a soft sucking sound before settling down again.

"I don't think I can sleep," Reese whispered on a sigh.

"Me, either."

Humming in the air between them was the memory of what they used to do to pass the time on sleepless nights. Reese felt her face grow warm, and her body turned liquid.

"Maybe I'll make myself a cup of chamomile tea," she said.

And even though he'd never been a tea-drinker, Duncan asked, "Want some company?"

She felt too vulnerable, too needy, for his company. Tell him no, she ordered. But her chin dipped in a nod. "Sure. That would be nice."

While she made the tea, Duncan built a fire in the living room's hearth. He'd pulled on a pair of wrinkled khakis and the striped polo shirt Reese had bought for him the Christmas before last. The scene when she entered the room with two stoneware mugs of the steaming herbal brew was decidedly domestic. And it was decidedly intimate since the flickering flames from the logs provided the only light.

She handed one of the mugs to him and they settled onto opposite ends of the sofa. On her side, Reese tucked her bare feet underneath the robe she'd pulled on over her pajamas. On his side, Duncan slouched down, put his heels on the coffee table and rested his head on the back cushion of the couch.

Reese had brought the monitor's receiver from her bedroom. It was plugged in to an outlet so they could hear Daniel if he started to fuss. And, even though they were far enough away from the nursery that they could have spoken in normal tones, they whispered.

Over the monitor came the sounds of grunting and rustling. They both sat up, put their feet on the floor. Then it stopped. They smiled a little sheepishly at one another and resumed their positions.

"You know, he's never really cried yet," Reese remarked. "Not when we saw him at the agency. Not during any of our visits with him at Maggie's house." After a sip of tea, she added, "I'm taking that as a good sign."

"He's had nothing to cry about. You pick him up, feed him or change him at the first sign of fussiness," Duncan pointed out.

"I don't want him to have to cry." It sounded silly, but it was true, she realized. She wanted him to be happy in his new home, with his new mother. She didn't want him to ever wonder if he would have been better off if his birth mother had chosen someone else.

"He's going to at some point, you know. That's what babies do, Reese."

"I know."

"It won't mean you're a bad mother. It won't mean his being here is a mistake."

She glanced over sharply. How was it possible he could still read her so easily when she still had such a hard time figuring him out?

"I didn't expect to feel this way," she admitted.

"What way?"

She took a sip of tea before admitting, "In way over my head."

"You're not."

"I thought I was ready for this and then when Maggie left today I felt so panicky," she said on a sigh. "It was all I could do not to stand on the porch and beg her to come back inside."

"I know."

He knew? "God, was it that obvious?"

He shook his head. "Only to me."

Their gazes connected, held. Reese swallowed. She took one of her hands off the mug and laid it on the empty cushion that separated them. Duncan reached out and covered it.

"What do I know about babies?" she asked after a moment.

He squeezed her hand. "You know what all new mothers know."

"And that's what…next to nothing?"

"What do you think? Giving birth doesn't mean they have any more knowledge. I think parenthood is kind of a learn-as-you-go thing."

"On-the-job training?"

"Uh-huh."

"But, God, Duncan, his very survival depends on me."

"Then he has nothing to worry about. You're doing fine." He squeezed her hand again, the pressure reassuring. "Remember, a lot of people far less competent and conscientious than you still manage to raise healthy, well-adjusted children."

She exhaled slowly. "I know. I keep telling myself that and my dad said as much when we talked on the telephone earlier today."

Duncan chuckled softly. "I can just hear him." Then he mimicked her dad's authoritative baritone. "If folks one step above barking can do it, Reesey, then surely you've got a good shot at it, too."

He'd always liked her father, she knew, as well as Wally Deerfield's colorful way of putting things.

"That's almost verbatim, by the way," she told him on a laugh.

"Well, if you won't believe me, then you should believe him. Your dad is one of the smartest people I know."

"He never went to school beyond high school," she reminded him. Duncan's father had earned an MBA from Harvard, as had Duncan.

"His level of education doesn't make him any less smart. A lot of people with doctorate degrees don't have your dad's common sense."

"That's true. I work with some of them." She sent him a sideways smile. "You know, my dad's always liked you."

"See. Smart man." His smile flashed. Then Duncan sipped his tea. Afterward, as he gazed into the cup, he admitted, "I want to be the kind of father he is."

"What do you mean?" Reese asked, but she thought she knew. Even though she reminded herself that it wouldn't affect her or Daniel, she nonetheless *hoped*, she knew.

"You know, approachable, involved. I want to be in the trenches." He glanced her way. "Not just getting reports from the people I hire to do the heavy lifting for me."

Like his father.

"I'm sure you'll be a great dad." She'd always believed that, which is what had made her infertility all the more painful. She'd felt so guilty, denying him what he could and should have had. Something some other woman could and someday would give him. "Maybe Breanna—"

"Don't. Not tonight." Duncan shook his head and pulled his hand away to shove it wearily through his hair. Afterward, he curved it around his mug. "Don't ruin tonight, Reese. Please."

"Okay."

But after that the conversation dried up and the silence that took its place was more strained than companionable. She finished off her tea and bid him good night.

An hour after she finally dropped off into a fitful sleep, Daniel awoke, hungry and wet. As she sat in the nursery's rocking chair and lulled him back to sleep, Reese swore she heard Duncan's footsteps in the hallway. The floorboards creaked and she waited, holding her breath and foolishly hoping, but he never came into the room.

It was just as well, she thought. What else was there to say tonight?

CHAPTER SEVEN

DUNCAN stood before the mirror in the guest bathroom and knotted his necktie. His stomach knotted as well. His parents were due to arrive any minute…unless they telephoned to reschedule. Again.

Today marked Daniel's second week in their home. Despite Duncan's parents' many promises, though, they hadn't made it over to see the baby yet. Duncan told himself it didn't matter. In fact, maybe it was even for the best that they showed little interest in being grandparents to this child since, ultimately, they wouldn't be. But when his mother had called to reschedule for the fourth time—she'd forgotten all about their plans to meet Lillian and Grant Sommers for dinner at the club—the ache in Duncan's chest had been as impossible to ignore as it was perplexing. Why should he care this much?

He told himself the disappointment he felt had nothing to do with their obvious disinterest in the baby. He just wanted to get this first visit out of the way. And, he supposed, it was the principle of the matter. Would it kill them to be supportive, to act interested, if only for his sake? After all, they didn't know that this was all just a big lie. Sometimes, Duncan had a hard time remembering that himself.

From down the hall, the sound of Reese's singing interrupted his thoughts. She didn't have the best voice, but she didn't let that stop her from warbling tunes from old Hollywood musicals. For some reason he'd always found her faulty pitch as endearing as her off-center smile. At the moment she was belting out "Somewhere Over the Rainbow."

She only sang when she was happy and it struck him then that it was a sound he hadn't heard in a very long time—not since the second miscarriage. He'd known of course that she wasn't happy. It had been one of the reasons he'd started staying late at work. He hadn't known what to do to help her. He hadn't known how to make their situation more tolerable. Facing her each night had meant facing his greatest failure.

It made it worse somehow that she'd wanted to give up on treatment, although she'd termed it "moving on." She'd wanted to go for counseling or to join an infertility support group. She'd wanted to adopt. He'd gone through the motions because she'd asked him to and he'd tried to find the same enthusiasm she obviously felt. He'd never managed it.

How could he when he'd just wanted to believe that their situation was a bad dream from which they both would awake eventually? Duncan's hands stilled and he frowned at his reflection. As he listened to Reese singing, it occurred to him that one of them had.

He followed the off-key lyrics and stood in the doorway of the nursery, his heart swelling painfully as he watched Reese dress Daniel on the changing table.

She'd already managed to get a T-shirt and diaper on him. No simple task that, given the way the baby wiggled and squirmed. Now she was working a small navy sweater over his head. Duncan told himself he was glad he didn't have to do it. The mere thought of maneuvering that bundle of moving body parts into a tiny outfit left him terrified, which made it all the more absurd that his fingers itched to try anyway.

Reese stopped singing and called out, "Where's Daniel? Where's my sweet baby?" When his small face was visible again, she exclaimed, "There he is! There he is!"

Afterward, she leaned down and sprinkled noisy kisses on Daniel's cheeks. The baby offered a toothless, watery grin in return, arms and legs pumping excitedly. Duncan swore he heard the beginnings of a laugh. Did babies start that already at just three months old? He stepped into the room for a closer look, wanting, for just a moment, to be part of the scene.

Her movements were slow but deft as she guided flailing appendages through armholes and into the legs of a pair of ridiculously small khaki pants. When she was done, she picked up the baby and nuzzled his neck.

"Not bad, huh, peanut?" she asked,

sounding rather pleased with herself. "I think I'm getting better at this."

She was finding her footing, he thought. Infertility and his mother's nagging had eroded her natural confidence, but some of it was returning at last. It made her all the more beautiful, all the more sexy, in his eyes. He swallowed and nearly groaned. Just what he needed. As if the past few weeks hadn't been torture already.

When she turned and spied him standing in the doorway, her smile faltered and she blinked. "Oh, hi."

"Hi."

Tilting her head to one side, she wrinkled her nose. "Just how long have you been standing there?"

"Long enough to catch part of the floor show, Miz Garland." He smiled as he said it, remembering the way he used to tease her about her singing.

"Very funny. I know I can't carry a tune, but Daniel doesn't seem to mind." She rubbed the baby's back in a gentle circular motion that was part pat, part caress. "Do you, peanut?"

"He's a captive audience."

Even though she glowered at him, humor lit up her dark eyes when she informed him airily, "No, he's nonjudgmental. He loves me just the way I am."

"Well, what's not to love?" Duncan's tone was soft and a little too serious. His response seemed to fluster her. She frowned and shifted the baby to her other hip as potent silence stretched.

Then it was her turn to fluster him. "Would…would you like to hold him while I finish putting on my makeup?"

More than anything.

And because it was true, Duncan shook his head.

"No! Um, thanks."

His response came out too quick, too curt. He watched Reese's face crumple and he wanted to kick himself. Hoping to soften his previous declaration, he added, "I mean, I'm sure he'll be fine in his crib for a few minutes. He really seems to like watching that mobile go around."

"He doesn't bite, you know."

"I know." Even so, Duncan stepped back into the hallway.

"But you don't want to hold him."

"No." His throat began to ache. "Sorry."

"There's no need to be." The corners of her mouth lifted into a smile that never quite reached her eyes. "I understand."

But she didn't. Indeed Duncan was only beginning to himself. He needed to keep his distance. Other than the first day at the agency, he had made a point of not holding the baby, finding excuse after excuse to avoid physical contact. Daniel felt too wonderful in his arms. He fit a little too perfectly there, snuggled up against Duncan's chest, burrowing with such ease into his busted up heart.

Is it so hard to pretend to love him, to want him?

Reese had asked him that the first night. The answer Duncan had come up with as he'd lain awake for the past several nights— listening for the baby and holding himself back from going to him when he heard Daniel start to fuss—was damning to say the least. No, it wasn't hard. It was too easy.

Where exactly did that leave Duncan? He was already losing Reese.

It was a relief when the doorbell chimed, announcing the arrival of his parents.

"I'd…I'd better go get that." He hitched a thumb over his shoulder in the general direction of the foyer and backed up a couple more steps.

Reese mustered up another smile, but she still looked sad. "Yes, you'd better."

"Reese—"

She shook her head, which was just as well. What could he say?

"Don't keep them waiting, Duncan. Daniel and I will be fine on our own."

And they would be, he thought.

In the living room, Louise and Grayson Newcastle sat side by side on the sofa, looking ill at ease despite their polite expressions. Duncan was seated on one of the chairs, one of his ankles rested on the opposite knee. The pose was casual, but his foot bobbed intermittently, making it impossible for him to completely mask his discomfort.

"The weather has been unseasonably cold lately," his father said.

Duncan nodded in agreement, glad to discuss the climate if that meant the silence would end. His mother, of course, was already shaking her head.

"It's always cold in February, Grayson," she contradicted. "I don't think this year is any different than the past sixty-six that you've lived in Michigan."

"Well, it seems to get colder every year."

Duncan thought his father was referring to more than the outdoor temperature with his comment.

His stomach began to burn in earnest. This promised to be a long and not particularly enjoyable visit. Few get-togethers with his parents were. He was used to stilted conversations and meaningless small talk. He'd grown up in a house that had all but echoed with both. Real feelings, raw emotions, those were things Duncan had learned early that one kept to oneself. Today, though, his parents seemed to be more reserved than ever. That is, until Reese entered the room holding the baby. Then, for just a moment, their aloofness lifted. His mother inhaled swiftly and, to Duncan's shock, she reached for his father's hand.

"Well, here he is," Reese said with forced gaiety. "This is Daniel. Daniel Ryan."

She turned the baby in her arms so they had a good view of his round, cherubic face. Duncan swore something akin to pain flickered in his mother's hazel eyes, there and gone before he could be sure he'd actually seen it at all.

"He's…he's a healthy-looking child," Louise said noncommittally. She released her husband's hand to fuss with the hem of her knee-length Chanel skirt.

"Yes," Grayson said stiffly. "Very healthy-looking."

Duncan saw Reese's smile thin and he felt the crushing weight of disappointment himself. Though he'd warned himself not to, and though he had told himself their indifference would be for the best in the long run, he'd hoped for a little more enthusiasm, he realized.

Duncan settled both of his feet on the floor and straightened in his seat.

"He is healthy," Reese said.

"For the time being." Louise continued to pluck at her hem and her gaze remained focused there.

Reese sighed. "Yes, but, the very same thing could be said—"

"Of any of us." Duncan finished her thought as he braced his arms on his knees.

"Exactly," Reese said, glancing over at him to nod.

She looked surprised. And no wonder. Just a couple of weeks ago during Jenny's initial visit, his thinking had been more in line with his mother's sentiment. What had caused him to change his mind? His gaze dipped to the baby, to that perfect little face that had stolen his breath on sight. He swallowed and sought the comfort of denial.

"But do you know anything about his people?" Louise asked.

It was all Duncan could do not to groan out loud. Did his mother always have to come across like such a snob?

"His *people* were young, unmarried and obviously unprepared to take on the responsibilities of parenthood," Reese replied through gritted teeth.

"Promiscuity is such a problem among the low-income," Louise tsked.

"I never said they were low-income, and,

what, wealthy people never hop into the sack before marriage?" Reese's voice rose.

Duncan cleared his throat. Hoping to defuse the explosion he knew was coming, he said, "According to the agency, the baby's birth parents were both college students."

That bit of information engaged his father's interest. "Oh? Do you know which university they attend? Is it one of the Big Ten schools?"

"Probably more like a community college." Louise snorted condescendingly.

"God!" Reese exclaimed. "How does his birth parents' choice of schools matter in the least?" Her tone was ripe with impatience and indignation.

"Really, Reese. There's no need to get so worked up," Louise admonished. "Duncan's father and I are just wondering what the two of you have been told about this child and his family's history. Such curiosity is natural, don't you think?"

"No, I don't. I think it would be natural for you to offer us your congratulations. I think it would be natural for you to make a fuss over the baby and to insist on holding him."

That's what most new grandparents would do. That's what her parents would be doing if they were here. How sad was it that the grandparents who were dying to see Daniel lived several states away, while the ones who lived just across town were less than enthusiastic? She inhaled through her teeth and let her breath out slowly. She was being ridiculous. The Newcastles' chilly restraint was for the best in this case. Besides, when was she going to finally accept that some things couldn't be changed?

Her gaze strayed to Duncan and memories taunted her. For a while, especially during the early years of their marriage, he had managed to shed his stuffiness and reserve. Over the past couple of weeks, she'd caught glimpses of the man she'd fallen in love with. He'd been home. He'd been engaged. Every now and then, she'd even found herself thinking—hoping almost—that things between them could be changed, repaired, and not just for Daniel's sake but for theirs.

The baby began to fuss. Reese lifted him to her shoulder. "Sorry, peanut," she murmured. "I didn't mean to upset you."

"No, you merely meant to insult us," Louise huffed.

"That wasn't my intention at all." No apology accompanied her statement, though. She wasn't in an apologizing mood right now.

Louise transferred her indignant gaze to Duncan. She always did that, Reese thought. She always tried to put him smack in the middle. In the past, Duncan had done his damnedest to stay neutral, often by copying his father's infuriating habit of ignoring Louise's biting remarks so as to avoid confrontation. That hadn't sat well with Reese.

"You need to take my side," she'd told her husband on more occasions than she cared to remember now.

This time Duncan did just that—literally. He rose from his chair and stood next to her. Reese struggled not to let her mouth fall open, especially when she heard his mother's tongue click in dismay.

Duncan cleared his throat. "Getting back to your question about the baby's history, Mother, we don't have a lot of information. Most of what we do know relates to the birth family's general health."

Louise's eyebrows arched. "And?"

Duncan glanced at Reese. He'd never looked over all of the information, so it was up to her to say, "One of his biological grandparents has hypertension, and a great-grandfather apparently had a stroke at an early age, but other than that..." She shrugged.

Louise pursed her lips and she nodded as if to say, "I told you so."

"Of course, high blood pressure runs in our family, too," Duncan added. "And didn't your uncle Bartholomew have a stroke, Father?"

"Heart attack, actually." Grayson's comment earned a withering look from his wife, and that was before he said, "He had his first one at forty-five and then a fatal one just before he turned sixty. That's one of the reasons my doctor has told me to limit my consumption of red meat."

Reese shot Duncan a quick look from beneath her lashes. He seemed to be suggesting that Daniel's DNA was irrelevant. He almost sounded as if he believed that. Yet not fifteen minutes earlier he had backed away when she'd asked him if he'd like to hold Daniel.

"What about their character? My mother always told me no amount of polish can wipe away the stain of bad blood," Louise said.

Reese felt her temper snap again. In as even a voice as she could manage, she said, "I believe the very fact that his birth parents loved him enough to place him for adoption says something about their character. They certainly had other options, other choices when they were confronted with an un-planned pregnancy. Making this choice required—"

"Selflessness," Duncan said. His gaze was thoughtful, maybe even a little pained, as he focused on the baby and added quietly, "Imagine the sacrifice involved in giving up something so precious."

Reese felt her eyes begin to sting and even as she called herself a fool, she shifted the baby to her other arm so she could reach for his hand.

"He is precious, isn't he?"

He didn't reply, but she swore the answer she longed to hear was shining in Duncan's blue eyes. If only he could love this baby then maybe…

"How do you know they won't change their minds? You read about that all the time," Louise warned.

Duncan cleared his throat and glanced back at his mother. "They've signed off on their rights. They have no legal claim to this child."

"So you've been told," she persisted. She shook her head and heaved a dramatic sigh. "I just hope you're not courting more heartache. God knows, you've been through enough of it already."

Because Louise's dire attitude had resurrected Reese's own sense of foreboding, she decided to change the subject.

"Daniel is such a good baby. He rarely cries or even fusses."

"Of course, Reese doesn't put him down often." One side of Duncan's mouth lifted as he said it and he squeezed her hand.

"You'll have to be careful or you'll spoil him," Louise cautioned, but she was looking at the baby now and some of the sternness had left her expression.

"Oh, I'm not worried about spoiling him." Reese let go of Duncan's hand so she could lift the baby to one shoulder. She dropped a kiss onto his head. "I'm enjoying him and I think he needs to know at this stage that he can count on me to see to all of his needs."

"Bonding," Duncan murmured.

It was the very thing he seemed determined not to do. Was that because he couldn't? Because he didn't want to?

Or could he be afraid?

"Yes, it's really important that children know they are loved and wanted," she said.

Duncan nodded, his gaze locked on the baby. She swore in that moment he looked so vulnerable, so…smitten. Before she could reconsider, she held Daniel out to him. "Take him while I go get the coffee, okay?"

His eyes grew wide and his mouth worked soundlessly for a moment, but he had no choice other than to accept the baby. He couldn't very well decline to hold him or to step away as he had earlier in the nursery. How would that look? She tried not to feel guilty for her high-handedness as she left the room, but she couldn't stop herself from questioning why she'd suddenly deemed it necessary.

In the kitchen, Reese poured coffee into four matching china cups and tried to settle her whirling emotions. She was being ridiculous. She chided herself for reading too much into Duncan's words and his expression. She was looking for things that weren't there. Expecting, maybe even hoping, that he would finally experience the same boundless love and joy she did whenever she looked at Daniel. But Duncan wasn't capable of feeling that way about an adopted baby. He'd told her that himself. She needed to remember it. She needed to accept it and move forward.

He had. He was.

But when Reese returned to the living room a moment later, the scene that greeted her almost had her dropping the tray of refreshments she carried. Duncan was seated on the couch between his parents with Daniel stretched out on his lap.

"He already sleeps six to eight hours straight each night," he was bragging. "And you should see him eat. This little guy is all business when you bring out a bottle of formula. He doesn't even like to take time out halfway through it to be burped."

Listening to him, those messy emotions began to swirl again. The china clattered and coffee splashed over the rims of the cups as she set the tray none too gently on the low table in front of them.

"Sorry," she mumbled.

As Reese mopped up the spilled liquid with a wad of napkins, Louise said nostalgically, "You were a fussy one, Duncan."

"I was?"

"Colic." She nodded. "Your nanny and I walked the floors with you for the first five months. It was…exhausting. I never thought I'd lose the circles under my eyes." She sighed then. "But when you would finally drop off to sleep, I would pull the rocking chair over next to the crib and just sit there, sometimes for an hour or more, so that I could look at you." She patted his cheek now in an uncharacteristic display of affection. "Oh, you were so beautiful."

"I do that," Reese admitted.

"Really?"

She nodded. Was it possible that after all this time she finally had something in common with her mother-in-law? "It's hard to imagine loving someone this much."

"It…it is." His mother blinked rapidly a few times. Then Louise pursed her lips. "Those napkins are dripping, Reese. Take care or you'll wind up with coffee stains on your rug."

The warm, fuzzy feeling proved fleeting. Reese set aside the soggy napkins and went into the kitchen to retrieve a dishrag. She returned just in time to hear Duncan ask his mother, "Do you want to hold him?"

The older woman straightened in her seat. Interestingly Louise looked almost eager for a moment, but then she shook her head and settled back against the cushions. "Oh, no. That's probably not a good idea. This blouse is silk."

"Daniel won't mind," Reese said.

Duncan sent Reese a grateful smile.

"Come on, Mother, take him," he said as he transferred the baby to her arms. Louise held Daniel awkwardly for a moment, before bringing him closer to her body.

On the other side of Duncan, his father murmured, "Take care to support his neck."

"I think I know how to hold an infant, Grayson." The words came out sharp-edged, but then Louise's expression mellowed and her tone turned soft with awe. "Oh, my. You forget how little they are."

She repositioned Daniel so that he was long ways in her lap and cupped his head in her hands. He wriggled and stretched, arms flailing, legs kicking, and issued a couple of squeaks that had everyone smiling.

"He's an active one," Grayson said. The corners of his mouth lifted, shifting the craggy lines of his face into a smile that could almost pass for doting.

Duncan didn't see it, though. He never took his eyes off the baby.

"Yes, sir. He can already hold up his head when he's lying on his belly. I know it's probably too early to tell, but something tells me he's going to be a natural athlete. He seems very coordinated. And smart. He's always so alert."

Reese studied Duncan. She swore she heard pride in his voice, in his words. She told herself it was manufactured. Surely it had to be. But it sounded so real, so sweet, that she took a moment to savor it anyway. Just as she savored the sight of her husband gazing in such wonder at her son while his usually aloof parents sat on either side of him, their interest fully engaged and focused on the baby.

On those long, dark nights when she had had only the dream of a child to keep her from slipping into the abyss of despair, this was how Reese imagined it could be.

Daniel disrupted the picture-perfect moment by spitting up. Some of the regurgitated formula ended up on the cuff of Louise's silk blouse.

"Oh. Oh, no. I was afraid that would happen." The older woman grimaced and quickly handed the baby back to Duncan. "I'd better put some water on that."

Her frown had returned and she looked as stern as ever when she rose from the sofa and hurried off in the direction of the bathroom. Louise's precious silk blouse might well be ruined, Reese thought with an inaudible sigh. The moment certainly was.

But then, she'd been foolish to allow herself to think it would last.

Duncan was unfazed by the mess. He was brushing the spit-up away from the corner of Daniel's mouth with the pad of his thumb. The baby had some spit-up on his outfit as well.

"Here, let me take him," she said. "I'll get him cleaned up. It's almost time for a nap anyway," she lied.

On the way to the nursery, she passed the bathroom. Louise hadn't closed the door all the way. It was open just far enough that Reese could see her mother-in-law's reflection in the oval mirror that hung above the sink.

Shock jolted through Reese. Louise's hands were over her face. Her shoulders were shaking, her entire body shuddering. She was crying. Even as Reese tried to tell herself it was a ruined blouse that caused the older woman's tears, she knew it wasn't.

Unnerved, she hurried past before she could be spotted.

Just before eleven, Reese decided to call it a night. After his parents left, Duncan had gone out as well. He'd returned a couple of hours ago, and was now in the guest room with the door closed. The sliver of light coming from beneath it told her he was still awake, though. She debated for a moment before knocking.

"Come in."

He was still fully dressed in khakis and a crew-neck sweater a few shades darker than his eyes. He was reclining against a couple of pillows he'd propped up against the headboard, a magazine on his lap, but it wasn't open. She looked for telltale signs of how and with whom he'd passed his evening, but she didn't see any.

"I'm going to bed," she said.

He nodded. "Did the baby go down okay?"

"Uh-huh."

"Good."

She waited, thinking he might say something more, but he didn't. His interest in the baby appeared to have waned, even though earlier it had seemed so real, so genuine. As had his mother's.

Reese debated telling him that she had seen Louise crying, but decided against it. It was such a private moment and, besides, she wasn't sure what it meant.

"Is there something else you wanted?" he asked pointedly.

I want to know why you went out tonight.

I want to know where you were.

I want to know why you're acting so distant right now.

She couldn't bring herself to say those things, though. Feeling awkward, she glanced around the room. "Do you have everything you need? I've…I've never asked."

"I'm not a damned guest, Reese."

His anger surprised her. What did he have to be in bad mood about?

"Spat with Breanna?" The question slipped out in a voice that had turned spiteful. She hated herself for it.

"Sure and then we had a sweaty round of makeup sex. That's what you want to hear, isn't it? That's what you're going to believe no matter what I say."

"Duncan—"

He shook his head and waved a hand toward the door. "Just go, okay? I'm really not in any mood for conversation right now."

Duncan saw her frown, as if his surliness left her puzzled. Didn't she know how hard today was for him? Couldn't she see how hard all of this was for him? Living with a wife who'd made it clear she didn't plan to stay married to him. Sharing his home with a baby who made him yearn not just for what he didn't have, but what he was beginning to realize he could have right now if the situation between he and Reese were different.

Is that what he wanted? Did he want to be Daniel's dad in more than name only?

The question had haunted him for the better part of the day, which was why he'd left right after his parents had. He'd needed to get away. He'd needed to think. Maybe, he could admit now, he'd even hoped to forget. A couple hours of smacking golf balls at a nearby enclosed driving range hadn't helped in the least. Several hours later all Duncan knew for sure was that he was lonely, sad, tired, frustrated and terribly confused.

He couldn't fault Reese for that. Not completely. Fairness demanded he claim some of the blame. So, when she started to withdraw from the room, he mumbled, "Sorry."

She stopped and studied him for a moment. "Me, too."

"I went to hit golf balls at the dome."

She nodded, looking as if she believed him, when she asked, "Still have that nasty slice?"

"No. It's a hook now."

"Want to talk about it?"

She wasn't referring to his golf stroke. "No."

"We used to talk about everything." She shook her head, looking bemused. "God, we used to stay up half the night talking when we were first married."

They'd stayed up half the night doing other things as well. No words had been necessary. Communication had been carried out through kisses and caresses. Memories stirred, beckoned, but he didn't want to recall them now.

His tone held accusation when he said, "Yeah, Reese, I know. But then you stopped listening to what I had to say."

She didn't deny it. Instead she nodded slowly. "I'm sorry for that."

Duncan scrubbed a hand down his face and blew out a frustrated breath. Some more of his foul mood leaked away. "Maybe I stopped listening to you, too."

Reese remained quiet for a long time. From the living room, he heard the wall clock chime out the hour. When it was silent again, she whispered, "It's not fair."

"What's not fair?"

"What infertility did to our marriage." She glanced down at her left hand as she said it and twirled the wedding band he'd placed there seven years earlier. His promise.

"No. It's not fair, but I don't think we can pin all of the blame on infertility."

"Maybe not."

"I wish…" Her words trailed off and she shook her head. "Never mind."

"What? Go on."

"It's going to sound crazy."

He sat up and swung his legs over the side of the bed. "What do you wish?"

"Well, of course, I wish we hadn't had to go through all of that heartache."

"Nothing crazy about that. I feel that way, too."

Her brow wrinkled and her eyes turned bright. "That's not what I mean."

"Then, what?"

"But I'm glad, too, because if we hadn't, Daniel wouldn't be here right now. Or, at least, he wouldn't be here with me. I wouldn't have this chance to be his mom." A tear leaked down her cheek. She brushed it away. "This final destination makes it hard to regret the journey, if you know what I mean."

Duncan swallowed, but his throat felt too tight to allow him to speak.

Reese took his silence to mean something else. "I told you it would sound crazy. What I just said probably doesn't make any sense to you."

"Reese," he began.

She waited, and he swore for just a moment she looked almost hopeful, but he couldn't continue. What had he planned to say? He wasn't sure. He couldn't seem to form a sentence, let alone a coherent thought. Finally he just shook his head and leaned back against the pillows.

"Well, good night, Duncan."

"Night."

CHAPTER EIGHT

Now that Duncan was back at work the following Monday and the days passed in a sleepless blur for Reese. Daniel's nose was stuffy and even though he wasn't running a fever and didn't have a cough, he fussed a lot and his whole schedule was thrown off. She was lucky if he slept three hours straight at night—and if she slept half that. During the day, if he took an hour-long nap it was a miracle, but instead of using the time to catch up on her own sleep, Reese found herself washing dishes or doing laundry. There seemed to be so much more of both these days.

She felt like a zombie, and she knew she didn't look much better. Plus, some of her newfound confidence had begun to ebb. Was Daniel unhappy? Was she a good parent?

What if she wasn't any better at being a mother than she was at being a wife?

At least Duncan wasn't working late. He arrived home at a reasonable time each day. It was a small comfort, though. He closeted himself in the den for the better part of the evening. What he did in there, Reese hadn't a clue. He didn't only close the door behind him, he locked it. He might as well have hung a sign from the knob that read: Do Not Disturb.

And so she didn't.

More than pride, practicality kept her from asking him for help. Ultimately she had to be able to care for Daniel on her own. Still, it wasn't only the workload she sometimes wanted to share or even her worries. It was the absolute wonder. She phoned Sara, her sister and her parents daily, eager to tell someone about Daniel's every facial expression and gurgling sound. They were enthusiastic listeners, but the sad fact remained, they were not Daniel's father.

More and more it began to bother her that Daniel didn't have one of those.

When the doorbell rang late Thursday

morning, Reese didn't want to answer it. It was just shy of noon, but she wasn't dressed, at least not in anything that she wanted to greet company wearing. Her hair was a mess and God only knew what her face looked like. She hadn't done more than splash cold water on it a few hours earlier. Those weren't the real reasons she didn't want to open the door, though. Her mother-in-law was on the other side.

After heaving a sigh of resignation, she forced her lips to curve into a smile and unbolted the lock, girding for the criticism that was sure to be forthcoming.

"Good morning, Louise."

"Hello, Reese."

"Please, come in out of the cold." She stepped back and held open the door.

As anticipated, the older woman's nose wrinkled as soon as she stepped into the foyer. Her gaze skimmed down Reese's yoga shirt and pants and stopped at her slippered feet. "It's nearly noon and you're not dressed. Aren't you feeling well?"

"I'm fine, but Daniel had a rough night and I wasn't expecting company." Reese pushed the tangled hair back from her face and stifled the urge to yawn.

To her surprise, Louise's cheeks turned pink and she appeared uncharacteristically contrite. "I'm sorry to just drop in like this. I know I should have called first."

"That's all right. I don't mind," Reese lied. "Can I take your coat?"

"Oh, I can't stay more than a minute or two. I'm meeting Irene Cornwall and Barbara Butterfield at the club for lunch in half an hour."

Reese worked up a look of disappointment even though she wanted to heave a sigh of relief. "Are you sure? I was just getting ready to make some tea."

It was easy to be courteous when she knew she wouldn't be taken up on her offer.

"Thank you, but no. I have something I wanted to drop off for the baby. I meant to bring it the other day when we came for a visit." She held out a small gift bag. Glancing past Reese, she asked, "Is Daniel awake?"

"Actually he just went down for a nap." After one hour of pacing up and down the hallway with him on one shoulder as Reese had sung every ballad and lullaby in her off-pitch repertoire.

"Oh." Louise frowned, looking oddly disappointed. Then she offered the bag to Reese. "I guess it doesn't matter. It's not as if he could unwrap a gift by himself anyway."

"Do you want me to wait for Duncan to get home to open it?" she asked politely.

"Oh, no. It's just…a little something."

From inside the folds of tissue paper, Reese pulled out a long-handled silver rattle. It was heavy enough to cause a head injury if the baby dropped it on himself. Just what every infant needed, she thought.

"Thank you, Louise. It's…lovely."

"I know you think it's foolish."

"No, I—"

"I did, too. It was Duncan's. It was a gift from Grayson's mother. Before Duncan, it belonged to Grayson. His grandmother gave it to him when he was born. It's been in the family for generations."

"Really." Reese eyed the rattle with new appreciation. It was an heirloom. As such it took on greater meaning. She couldn't help but wonder if by giving it to Daniel Louise was saying that she accepted him. Would that be a good thing? It took an effort not to frown when she added, "I'll be sure to put it someplace safe."

"Someday you can pass it on to your first grandchild. You know how we Newcastles like our traditions." Louise laughed a little self-consciously.

Reese's eyes began to sting as a confusing eddy of emotions swirled. This was one she actually would be glad to help continue if the circumstances were different. "Thank you."

"Do…do you think you and Duncan will try to have other children?"

The question caught her off guard and so her mouth gaped open for a moment before she recovered. "Do you mean will we adopt more?"

Louise nodded, but then added, "Or maybe you'll get pregnant on your own now and you won't lose the baby. You hear about that happening all the time after couples adopt. They wind up having children of their own."

Louise wasn't the first person to mention

this phenomenon to Reese. Everybody seemed to know somebody who knew somebody whom this had happened to.

"Daniel is my own."

"Yes. You know what I mean."

Reese swallowed a sigh. She wanted to make it clear she hadn't turned to adoption as some sort of noninvasive fertility treatment option.

"I don't think my reproductive problems went away just because we got Daniel."

Louise looked disappointed. "I suppose not."

"I'd like for him to have siblings someday, though," Reese said. She didn't know how she would accomplish that, only that it was true.

"I always wanted more than one child. We thought a couple of times, but..." Louise shrugged delicately and glanced away. "It just wasn't meant to be, though, and we didn't have all of the medical options available to us that couples have today."

The revelation had Reese blinking. "I didn't realize that you... You never said anything."

Louise waved a hand in dismissal. "It's

not something women of my generation and station talked openly about with other people. In any event, it was a long time ago."

Yet she didn't seem to be over it. Of course, Reese knew better than anyone that infertility and miscarriages were things that one never really "got over."

A thought clicked into place then. "Did you and Grayson ever think about adopting?"

"Good heavens, no. I mean, not *seriously* at any rate." She fussed with her scarf, her expression growing austere. "Besides, we already had Duncan. Sometimes you just have to be happy with what you have and stop chasing after what you don't."

Reese wasn't sure why, but she thought Louise's reply sounded like something she'd been told rather than a conclusion she had reached on her own.

She decided to let it go, though. "I suppose."

Daniel began to cry and Reese sighed heavily as she glanced at her wristwatch. "Well, that nap lasted all of twenty minutes."

She expected her mother-in-law to say her farewells and go. After all, Louise had said she was meeting friends at the club for lunch. Instead of leaving, though, she was asking, "Would you mind if I peeked in on him?"

"Um, no. Of course not."

As they started down the hallway, Louise said, "You mentioned that he had a rough night."

"Yes, he's been fussy for the past few days. Neither one of us is getting much sleep at night."

"And you haven't taken him to see the doctor?" More than criticism, Louise's voice held what sounded like concern. Hearing it stoked Reese's own insecurities back to life.

Her tone was defensive when she replied, "I called the pediatrician's office and talked with the nurse yesterday. She said since Daniel isn't lethargic and still has an appetite that I should give it another day or two before bringing him in. She said even though he's not quite four months old he could be teething already."

Louise pursed her lips. "Teething? Duncan didn't cut his first teeth until he was nearly seven months old."

Reese gripped her hands together. "I've

heard that some babies are born with teeth. He does seem to be drooling a lot and his nose is running."

Please, she prayed silently. Please let it just be teeth and not something I've done or not done right. She couldn't help recalling what a happy, healthy and content baby Daniel had been mere days ago.

Never one to freely offer comfort and reassurance, Louise said, "Given how little you and Duncan know about the baby and his people, I think you should take him to the doctor for a full physical. They can run tests for a lot of inherited conditions these days."

"There's nothing wrong with my son!" Reese snapped. Stress and fatigue had her eyes filling, her throat aching. In the nursery, she picked up Daniel from his crib and cradled him in her arms. They were both crying when she said, "God, I think it's me. I think the problem is me."

"What ever do you mean?"

Reese swiped at the tears that were gathering on her lower lashes, but more took their place. She felt so defeated, so beaten, that she found herself admitting to her mother-in-law of all people what she had told no one else. "I think he might…I think he might miss his foster mother."

"Nonsense."

"It's not nonsense. Maybe God knew I wouldn't be any good at mothering and so he opted not to give me children." That possibility had kept her awake the past few nights even more so than Daniel's fussiness. And she'd found herself wishing she could seek Duncan's counsel and comfort.

"Nonsense," Louise said again.

"Of course you would think so. You find it so much easier to believe there's something wrong with him."

"I didn't mean to imply—"

"But you did, Louise." Reese shook her head then, angrier with herself than she was with Duncan's mother. "I'm sorry. I'm…I'm just tired."

And lonely.

And riddled with doubts and second thoughts—not just about her parenting skills, but about the divorce she had promised Duncan.

Louise tilted her head sympathetically. "I

can see that you're out of sorts and exhausted. You have dark circles under your eyes."

Of course her mother-in-law would point out those. "As I said, I haven't been getting the recommended eight hours."

"You know, you really should hire a nanny. I could ask around at the club for some recommendations, if you'd like. Believe me, an extra set of hands is an absolute godsend when it comes to raising children. I couldn't have done it without some help."

Reese was beginning to feel that way, too. "I'll think about it," she lied as a sob lodged in her throat.

After Louise left, it made her all the more miserable to realize just how much she wanted that extra set of hands to belong to Duncan.

Reese was sitting at the table eating a bowl of cereal and reading the newspaper when Duncan entered the kitchen that evening. She'd taken the advice of the nurse at the pediatrician's office and given Daniel some pain reliever. He was napping. It was dinner-time, but she hadn't bothered to cook a meal. It seemed like too much trouble when she and Duncan weren't eating together anyway.

He pointed to the newspaper. "Mind if I take the sports section?" They were the first words he'd spoken to her since the "hello" he'd offered when he'd arrived home an hour earlier.

"Be my guest."

He picked it up and started toward the door, but then he halted. Turning he said, "My mom called me at the office earlier. She, um, mentioned that she stopped in today for a brief visit."

"Yes." Reese set her spoon down and pushed the bowl aside, her appetite gone. "She dropped off a gift for Daniel. A sterling silver rattle. It's been in your family for generations apparently."

"Really?" He sounded as surprised as Reese felt.

"Uh-huh. Shocked me, too. I think the baby's growing on her." She said it light-heartedly, but neither of them laughed.

In fact, Duncan frowned. "She said she

thought you could use the help of a competent nanny."

Reese rolled her eyes. "Yes, well, what single mother couldn't?"

His frown intensified and he tugged at the hair just above his collar. "I...I know I haven't been particularly helpful this past week—"

"Particularly helpful?" She shook her head at the stunning understatement. "When you're home you've been missing in action." She pointed to her cereal bowl. "We don't even eat together. If not for running across your dishes in the kitchen sink, I'd be wondering if you'd moved out again."

Color splotched his cheeks. "I'm sorry."

"No." She blew out a breath and shook her head. "I'm sorry. That was unfair. Our deal didn't include diaper duty or anything like that."

"Our deal." His mouth twisted.

Reese decided to change the subject. "Jenny called today. She'll be by next Wednesday for a home visit. Can you be home at five o'clock?"

"Sure." He shrugged.

"She wanted to know how everything is

going. You know, how we're settling into parenthood."

His brows rose. "What did you tell her?"

"I told her that we're one big happy family and that everything is great."

"Yeah. Just great." The sarcasm in his tone matched that which had been in hers.

She decided to change the subject again. "Did you know your mom wanted more children after you were born?"

His forehead furrowed. "No. I...I just assumed..." He shrugged. "How do you know?"

"She mentioned it today."

"She actually told you that?"

"Yes. You know, from some of the other things she said I got the feeling that she and your father may have considered adoption."

"My parents?" he said incredulously.

She nodded. "I think they were pressured not to pursue it."

Duncan ran a hand through his hair. "That I would believe. Both of my grandmothers could be very close-minded."

"The apple didn't fall far from the tree."

He scowled. This time, he was the one

who changed the subject. "Mother didn't mention that she'd given you the rattle. It's a family heirloom, you know. A Newcastle tradition."

"I won't keep it, if that's what you're worried about."

"I'm more worried about her getting attached to the baby," he snapped. "God, Reese, I know you think my mother's heart is carved out of stone, but it would kill her to fall in love with that baby only to find out she won't be part of his life. That she won't be seeing him grow up."

Reese thought of the vulnerability she'd glimpsed beneath her mother-in-law's otherwise domineering facade when Louise had alluded to her own fertility troubles.

"I don't want to see your mother hurt."

"What about me?" he asked quietly and at that moment he looked vulnerable, too. "My heart's not carved out of stone, either, you know."

Her pulse began to pound. Just what was he saying? "Duncan?"

"The apple doesn't fall far from the tree, remember?" Then he shook his head and all traces of vulnerability vanished. "Good night."

Newspaper in hand, he headed in the direction of the den. In the quiet house Reese heard the heavy oak door close and then the lock clicked.

Duncan sat on the love seat in the den and willed the time to pass until he could call it a night and go to bed. The past week had been sheer torture. Every hour he was at work, he wanted to be home. He missed being with Reese. Even more damning, he missed being with the baby. He'd picked up the telephone in his office a dozen times each day, thinking up plausible excuses for calling his wife. Did she need him to pick anything up at the store on his way home? Was everything okay? How was Daniel feeling?

He knew, of course, that neither of she nor the baby had been sleeping much. He hadn't been sleeping much, either. He'd lain awake in the guest room, listening as Reese paced up and down the hallway, but he hadn't gone to help her. Nor had he called her from work. As much as he wanted to, he couldn't. Just as when he was home, he couldn't spend time with her and the baby.

Missing in action, she'd said. Well, he saw it as self-preservation. He was holding himself separate, hoping that distance would be an effective barrier against even greater heartache and rejection. The dull throbbing in his chest told him it wasn't working. Even so, he sat alone in a den as another evening stretched out before him, and tried to pretend he wasn't dying inside.

CHAPTER NINE

FOR the next several days Daniel remained fussy and he still was not sleeping soundly at night, but Reese was no longer quite so worried. He had a bottom tooth. It hadn't poked all the way through yet, but from the look of the baby's red and swollen lower gum it appeared another one was on its way.

"I'd be cranky, too," she said as she held a frozen washcloth to his mouth for him to chew on.

It was a trick her mother had told her about during one of their daily telephone conversations. Like Louise, Maureen had dismissed Reese's concerns about the baby not bonding with Reese as nonsense. Coming from her own mother, the declaration had carried much more weight.

"I'm sorry I took your bad mood personally," she told Daniel now. "It was fatigue talking, and I guess I'm still a little nervous about being a mom. Am I doing okay, peanut? Are you happy with me?"

Daniel flapped his arms and squealed enthusiastically as he gummed the washcloth. Reese felt her world tilt back onto its axis. The sense of rightness expanded a little when Duncan called just after noon.

"Duncan. Hi. This is a surprise."

He cleared his throat, not sounding entirely comfortable when he admitted, "I've been thinking about you a lot lately."

"Oh?"

"Yeah."

Reese cleared her throat. She wasn't entirely comfortable either when she admitted, "I've been thinking about you, too."

Neither of them said anything for a long moment, although she could hear his breathing and she supposed he could hear hers as well.

"We've made a real mess of things, Reese," he said at last.

She pressed her lips together tightly. "Mmm-hmm."

"What are we going to do about it?"

Her heart hitched. "Wh-what do you mean?"

"I don't think we can go on like this for several more months. I know I sure as hell can't."

She experienced a moment of paralyzing panic. "But you said you would do this for me. You agreed."

"Reese—"

She cut him off. "You know what will happen if you move out before the adoption is final. Once the people at the agency get wind of it, they'll take Daniel. God, Duncan, I can't give him back now. He's my son. Don't you understand? *He's mine.*"

Ominous silence greeted her declaration. Finally, he murmured, "I'm not saying I want to leave again."

"Then what are you saying?" Reese managed to ask, even though her voice cracked and her hands were still shaking.

"I don't know." He sighed heavily. "We need to figure out a solution together."

Together. She couldn't help feeling it was a promising word choice.

Then Duncan was saying, "I don't have time to go into it now. Besides, this is something that needs to be discussed face-to-face rather than over the telephone."

He was right, of course. "Okay."

"I'll be home my usual time."

"Maybe we can have dinner together," she suggested.

"I'd like that, Reese."

"Me too." Her voice was barely above a whisper.

"What was that?"

"I said, me too."

"Yeah?"

He sounded so surprised—hopeful?—that she couldn't help smiling, even though for some reason her eyes filled with tears. "Yeah."

When he spoke again, he changed the subject. "It sounded like you had another long night last night."

"Daniel was up a lot."

"How's the, um, *big guy* doing?"

The use of a nickname had her heart melting a little more and some of her apprehension ebbed. "Do you mean the peanut?"

Duncan snorted out a laugh. "Call him that and you'll give the kid an inferiority complex."

"I'll be sure to come up with a different nickname before he goes to high school," she replied dryly. Then, more seriously, she added, "Daniel seems to be doing better this morning. He finally cut a tooth."

"A tooth. Really?"

"Yep. The bad news is another one appears to be on the way."

"Jeez, poor kid. At this rate he'll have a mouthful by the time he turns one."

"I don't know about a whole mouthful. I'm just relieved to know this was why he's been so restless and crabby. For a while there I thought... Never mind."

"No, what?"

Reese shifted the receiver to her other ear. "It's stupid."

"Come on, Reese. You can tell me."

And she knew she could. At that moment, she knew that more than anyone else in the world, Duncan would understand perfectly.

"I thought he was pining for his foster mom or birth mother or whoever."

"Nah. Never. Just your nerves. Given everything we went through, it's not all that surprising that you'd have doubts now that the baby is here."

"Sometimes it still seems too good to be true," she said.

"But it's not. It's real."

"I know. Still, for a while there I was worried that he didn't want me."

"That's not possible," he stated with quiet conviction. Duncan raised gooseflesh on her arms when he added, "If it were, I wouldn't be crabby and restless all the time."

The unexpected comment sent heat spiraling up her spine and stoked forbidden yearnings back to life.

"See you this evening," he said before hanging up.

What would that evening bring? Reese wondered as she listened to the drone of the dial tone. He said he didn't want to move out again. He said they needed to work out a solution together. She laid a hand to her hammering heart and considered another possibility: reconciliation.

Is that what he wanted? More to the point, is that what *she* wanted?

Reese told herself she wasn't sure, but that didn't stop her from hopping in the shower when Daniel went down for his nap. She wanted to feel fresh and look attractive. Maybe she would even wear her hair down for a change and apply some makeup to highlight her eyes and hide the dark circles underneath them.

A couple of hours later, she was just bundling the baby up for a trip to the grocery store when the phone rang. It was Duncan again.

"Hi Reese."

"Hi. Wow. This makes twice in one day." She laughed, feeling oddly self-conscious as she played with the ends of her unbound hair.

"I used to call you more often than that."

She remembered. "You'd leave messages on my voice-mail at school." Some of them had been suggestive enough to have her glancing around, afraid a colleague or student might overhear his racy comments.

"You used to call me back," he said quietly.

She remembered that, too. Their phone calls had become less frequent over the years. They'd stopped entirely several months ago. Daniel gurgled, dragging Reese back to the present.

"I was just getting ready to run to the store to pick up some groceries. We don't have much of anything around here. Do you have something in particular you'd like for dinner?"

He cleared his throat. "Actually, that's why I'm calling. I'm afraid I have some bad news. I've got a meeting at five o'clock."

She stopped fidgeting with her hair and tucked it behind her ear. "Today?"

"Yes. It came up rather suddenly."

"I guess so." She willed the disappointment from her tone and tried to stay upbeat. "Well, what time will you be home? I can hold off on dinner."

"The thing is, I don't know what time I'll be through. The meeting is going to take at least a couple of hours. We're teleconferencing with our counterparts at a sister institution in California. Afterward, we're having a management meeting."

"Hmm, sounds important."

"It is or I wouldn't be staying late. I'm sorry, Reese."

"You must have had a lot of important meetings over the past year." She couldn't help it, her tone had turned chilly.

Duncan sighed. "Don't do that. Please."

"Do what?" she asked. "I'm just stating fact."

"I'd reschedule if I could."

"It's no big deal, Duncan. Really. Saves me a trip to the grocery store this afternoon."

"It's business, Reese. *Only* business."

Did he sound defensive? Guilty? The old doubt throbbed like a bad tooth. "No need to apologize or to explain," she said crisply.

"Reese—"

But she hung up. Afterward, she called herself a dozen kinds of fool for thinking that things between them could change.

Reese was curled up on the couch reading a book when Duncan got home. It was just before eight o'clock, but she looked exhausted...and beautiful. Her hair was down, her eyes illuminated with some sort of cosmetic magic that made them appear larger and more inviting.

But she wasn't smiling. No. It didn't take

more than a glance to realize she wasn't happy to see him.

"Hi." He tucked his hands into the front pockets of his trousers.

"Hi."

"Baby sleeping?" he asked, nodding toward the hall.

"For now."

"Did you eat? I stopped at Tony's and picked up a pizza on the way home. Pepperoni and mushroom, your favorite."

She shook her head. "That's okay. I had some toast about an hour ago."

"Sorry. I should have called to let you know I was thinking about stopping somewhere."

She waved a hand. "It doesn't matter."

Her tone suggested she was referring to more than what she'd had for dinner. God, they forever seemed to be sliding back to square one.

"I'm sorry about the meeting."

"It's okay."

"No. You're mad."

Reese set aside her book and changed the subject. "You know, the baby shower is coming up next weekend. My parents called tonight. They will be arriving on Thursday and they plan to stay through Monday. They're eager to see Daniel."

"I'm sure they are."

"Um, there's just one little problem."

"What?" he asked cautiously.

"Well, they'll be staying…here. In our guest room. We need to talk about where you will be sleeping."

"Where do you want me to sleep?" He meant it as a challenge.

Reese tilted up her chin. "My bed is off limits."

"*Our* bed," he corrected.

"Off limits," she repeated.

"You're not suggesting that I should sleep on the couch during their stay?"

"No."

"Then that leaves one option."

She crossed her arms over her chest, and Duncan figured her body language told him just what she thought of the idea of sharing a bed with him.

"Sorry that would be such a hardship for you," he drawled. "Maybe I can pretend to have a meeting out of town during their visit and get my old room back at the Hilton."

That had her blinking. "You were at the Hilton?"

"I don't expect you to believe that, but yes. And I was by myself the entire time." He closed his eyes. "Just like tonight I was at a meeting that ran late. And before you ask, yes, Breanna was there. All of the bank's top management was. God, I'm so tired of this. I'm so damned tired of defending myself when I've done nothing." He raked a hand through his hair. "Nothing!"

"I'm tired of it, too." She rose to her feet. "I don't want to fight about it anymore."

He took no pleasure in the fact that she looked miserable and worn out. "Then what do you want?" he asked.

She rubbed her eyes, smudging her makeup. She still looked beautiful. "Way more than I have a right to at this point."

That was an interesting rejoinder. When she started past Duncan, he reached out to clasp her upper arm. "What do you mean by that?"

"Nothing."

"It's not nothing."

"Duncan…" She shook her head.

"Talk to me. Tell me." He pulled her closer and his tone grew more insistent when he whispered against her cheek, "It's not nothing, Reese. It's something. It's got to be something, because nothing doesn't make people feel like this."

"Don't, Duncan. Don't do this to me, okay?" The words were a near-sob, but she didn't pull away. Instead she leaned against him and held on as the breath shuddered in and out of her lungs.

"What am I doing?" he asked.

"You're confusing me."

"I'm confused, too, Reese."

"About me?" She straightened and then moistened her lips. "Or about the baby? We're a package deal now. One comes with the other."

"Don't you think I know that?"

She did pull away then. Stepping back, she tucked her rioting hair behind her ears. "I'm too tired to think."

"Then don't. Maybe you should just let yourself feel." He settled his hands on her elbows and drew her forward again until their hips bumped and their bodies were flush. He framed her face with his hands, stroked her cheeks with his thumbs. "It used to be so good between us."

"That was a long time ago."

"Not so long that I've forgotten. Let's see if I can help you remember." He tilted up her face to receive his kiss. His mouth moved against her slowly, gently, as memories spun out from the past and collided head-on with his current need.

Reese moaned. It was all the encouragement he needed. The kiss picked up in tempo and hands were added to the equation. Not just his hands, but hers. They skimmed eagerly over his clothed skin before working their way underneath fabric. His suit coat was shed along with his tie, after which she turned her attention to the buttons running down the front of his shirt. He nuzzled her neck as she struggled with them, offering encouragement with a string of kisses that ended just below her ear.

When she finally finished and his shirt joined his other clothes on the floor, it was his turn. He tugged the sweater she wore over her head. Then he groaned aloud at the sight she made standing before him in a flirty, thin-strapped T-shirt that hugged her slim torso like a second skin. She wasn't wearing a bra. Her hair was a tumbled, tawny mess that waved around her shoulders and her complexion glowed like porcelain in the lamplight.

"God, you're beautiful."

He reached for the hem of her T-shirt and, pulse pounding like a jackhammer, he began to work it up. His knuckles had just grazed the underside of her breasts when she stopped him.

Even with need screaming and hormones zinging through her system like lightning bolts, Reese came to her senses. She stilled Duncan's hands, held them between hers almost as if praying. And in a way she was. For strength.

"This isn't the answer," she said in a shaky whisper.

"No?"

"This is sex, Duncan. It's not going to solve our problems."

He yanked his hands free and issued an oath. "It might not solve all of our problems, but it's not just sex. Not for me. It's never been just sex for me. It's always been making love. Even when it became mechanical and dictated by basal thermometer readings, I still thought of it as making love." He glared at her. "Do you know why?"

She opened her mouth, but no words came out.

"Because it was with you, Reese. It was with you."

The declaration was so fierce and so sincere that it made her eyes burn, her throat ache. "Oh, Duncan."

She reached out a hand to him, but he backed up and shook his head.

"Do you trust me?" he demanded sharply.

She swallowed and felt her heart flutter when she told him, "I want to."

"That's not good enough, Reese. You either do or you don't." He reached into the pile of clothes on the floor for his shirt. Shrugging into it, he added, "You either believe that I've been faithful to you and kept the vows I made on our wedding day or you

don't. And if you don't, if you can't, then—
God!—there's no hope for us."

"Do you want there to be?"

"What do you think? I love you. I've never
stopped loving you."

"Daniel—"

"Yes, Reese, think about Daniel. Think
about what that baby really needs."

With that, he stalked off down the hall.
After he was gone, Reese felt chilled. She
donned her sweater and huddled on the
couch with her knees pulled up to her chest,
but she couldn't get warm. Nor could she
make her thoughts settle. More than
confused, she felt bewildered. There hadn't
been only anger in Duncan's voice or even
resignation. He'd sounded destroyed and
desperate. It was those things that forced her
to reexamine the conclusion she'd previously
reached about his faithfulness. A conclusion
that she had found herself starting to
question ever since Daniel's arrival.

She forced herself to think back objec-
tively on the many arguments she and
Duncan had had about Breanna Devin. Arguments that Reese had instigated. She

recalled the vicious accusations she'd hurled at him and his strident protestations of innocence. She recalled his outrage, his wounded expression, and finally the silence that she had taken as an admission of guilt.

But was it?

Indeed, what evidence of an affair had she ever had beyond his late nights at the office and his taciturn moods?

Yes, they'd stopped talking and they'd stopped touching, but she'd never stumbled across any telltale receipts or answered the telephone to suspicious silence. Had Reese needed to believe there was another woman because that had made it easier to understand his absences and to accept his emotional withdrawal?

Do you trust me? he'd asked a moment ago. She swallowed, feeling queasy as a bitter irony presented itself. Maybe *she* was the person she hadn't trusted. Maybe *she* was the person in whom she'd lost faith.

When she stopped outside his bedroom an hour later, no light shot from under the door. He was asleep or at least wanted her to believe that. Just as well, she decided, continuing down the hall. She needed to tread carefully and figure out exactly what to say.

It snowed overnight. Duncan was already up and shoveling the drifts that blocked the driveway when Reese got out of bed just before nine o'clock on Saturday morning. Daniel had awoken three times during the night, but that wasn't the only reason she felt so groggy. Even when the baby had slept she'd lain awake thinking about Duncan. He was just down the hall, so close and as far away as ever.

She'd wanted to go to him. She owed him an apology for doubting him, for so unfairly accusing him. That much was clear. The rest was still a bit murky since they had yet to speak of the future or to discuss the past, two things Reese knew were necessary to move forward. He'd told her that he loved her, but he hadn't included Daniel in that declaration.

Could he love him? She needed to be positive on that score. Everything hinged on that.

"He has to," she whispered to the baby as he finished his formula. "He just has to."

Daniel fussed when she pulled away the bottle. He'd only gotten four ounces. It was all the formula that was left. Despite the weather, a trip to the grocery was obviously in order. Reese really should have gone the day before, but she'd been too disappointed after Duncan's call to make the trip. Now it was an utter necessity. In addition to formula, Daniel was running low on diapers and wipes, and the refrigerator shelves were bare except for a block of partly molded cheddar, a bag of dried out baby carrots and the usual assortment of condiments.

Reese burped Daniel and got them both dressed. She was putting the baby into his carrier seat when the back door opened and Duncan came in from their home's attached garage.

His cheeks glowed red from cold and exertion, and his hair was a sexy mess. He didn't wear blue jeans often, but he had on a pair today. He wore them well, she thought. He wore everything well. A needle of awareness poked through her nerves and exhaustion as she remembered a little too vividly how they had peeled off one another's clothes the night before.

They eyed one another warily for a moment before Reese finally said, "Good morning."

"Morning."

"I see that it snowed."

"About six inches. Are you going out?" he asked, stamping the excess white stuff off his boots.

"Yes. I need to go to the grocery store."

"With the baby?" The question was unnecessary since she was buckling Daniel into the carrier even as he asked it.

"Uh-huh."

He frowned. "Roads haven't all been plowed and some of the intersections might be slippery."

"I'll brake early and often," Reese replied around a yawn.

When she glanced back at Duncan, he was still frowning. "Are you awake enough to drive?"

"I'm fine. I just could use some coffee, but, of course, we're out of that. We're out of just about everything. In fact, a few more diaper changes and Daniel will be going alfresco." She forced herself to laugh.

Duncan didn't laugh. He studied her face. "Are we going to talk about this, or are we just going to keep on pretending?" He pulled off his gloves and unzipped his jacket.

Reese zipped hers up and cleared her throat. "We'll talk about it. I promise. There are a lot of things I need to say to you."

"But?"

"But right now I need to go to the store. Daniel only got four ounces of formula. He's not going to stay content for long."

"So, we'll talk when you get back?"

She nodded slowly. "When I get back."

He sighed, clearly not happy with the postponement. "Well, be sure to keep an eye out for other drivers. You know how stupid some people are when the roads are slick."

"I'll drive defensively," she promised, feeling a little nervous now about taking the baby out. "It's less than three miles each way to the grocery store," she rationalized.

Hoisting the carrier, she started for the door, but Duncan didn't move out of her way. Instead, he covered her fingers on the handle.

"At least wait until this afternoon. The salt trucks and plows will have all the roads clear by then."

"It's sweet of you to worry about me," she whispered.

"I'm worried about *both* of you," he corrected.

Something in his tone had her heart lurching. "Why don't you come with us, then?"

She was as surprised as Duncan by the offer, but he hesitated only a moment before zipping up his coat and pulling back on his gloves.

"We'll take my car. It handles better in snow."

"And on the way maybe we could stop—"

"At Starbucks?" he finished, taking the carrier from her hands.

She smiled. "Yes."

"I'm dying for a cup of coffee," they both said at the same time.

Duncan pushed the cart down the grocery store aisles as Reese loaded it with the items from her list. The basket was filling fast, especially since the front of it was taken up with the baby's carrier.

Daniel was awake and he watched Duncan intently. It had been nearly two weeks since he'd held the baby, touched him. He'd hoped that absence would somehow lessen the foothold Daniel already had in his heart. What a foolish, foolish wish, he thought now.

Have you missed me?

The baby cooed, as if he'd somehow heard the unasked question. It was impossible not to smile at him, impossible not to reach out and tickle his chin. Daniel grinned in return.

When Reese stepped away to weigh a bunch of grapes, Duncan said softly, "Hey, big guy. How have you been?"

Daniel grinned again and began to babble happily. His legs kicked beneath the blanket and his small hands bunched and began to flail.

"I'm glad to see you, too."

"Oh, isn't he adorable," an older woman said. Stopping her cart next to theirs, she smiled at Duncan. "How old is your son?"

"He's not..." His gaze cut back to the baby and he felt his heart tremble, and then it tumbled all the way. What determined the perimeters of his and Daniel's relationship? Was it simply a matter of genetics? He knew from personal experience what an imperfect bond that could create. Or was it measured in something less quantifiable, yet more definitive? Something like love? Duncan was finally sure of the answer. "My son is not quite sixteen weeks."

When he glanced up, Reese had returned to the cart. She held a bag of grapes in one hand. Her dark eyes regarded him solemnly.

"Our son," she said in a raspy whisper.

"Our son," he agreed.

"Just admiring your beautiful baby," the woman told her. "You and your husband sure have yourselves a keeper."

"Daniel is that," Reese replied.

Duncan nodded, too, as emotions he no longer wanted to deny welled up inside him and then spilled over.

"You certainly got your figure back quickly," the older woman said to Reese. She patted her own plump middle and chuckled. "I'm still carrying around some of the weight I gained with my boys and the youngest is thirty now. You don't even look like you've ever been pregnant."

Most women would have enjoyed the compliment. Reese colored and stammered, "I…um, Daniel is…"

Duncan leaned over and kissed her, effectively stopping her from finishing whatever explanation she planned to offer.

"My wife looks fantastic, doesn't she?"

He felt his heart knock out an extra beat when she offered up the off-center smile that had so long ago sealed his fate.

"Hmm," the older woman murmured with a knowing grin. "I think this baby is likely to have a little brother or sister in his future. Or maybe one of each given the way you two are looking at one another right now."

Reese blushed. "We always wanted—"

"Three," Duncan finished.

CHAPTER TEN

WHEN they got home, Reese unbundled Daniel and fed him a few more ounces of formula as Duncan unloaded their groceries and put them away. The baby fell asleep almost immediately after eating, apparently done in by his first family outing. She laid him in the crib and joined her husband in the kitchen, where he was making a sandwich.

"Duncan?"

He smiled at her over his shoulder. "Want one? It's a Dagwood special."

"Not right now. I thought…I thought we could talk."

He turned and his expression sobered. "All right."

The floor was hers, but where to begin? She decided to start with one irrefutable fact.

"First, I want you to know I love you."

His smile was hesitant. "But?"

She shook her head. "There's no 'but' when it comes to that." For emphasis, she repeated, "I love you, Duncan."

She watched him swallow. "Okay, so, we love one another. There's still more to our marital problems than that."

"I know." Reese walked to the stove and turned on the burner beneath the teakettle as she let her mind stretch back to the time she'd tried her damnedest to forget. "You know, the first time I met Breanna was just after we'd lost the second baby. I came up to your office to meet you for lunch and she was there."

He swore half-under his breath. "We *work* together, Reese."

"I'm not making accusations. I'm trying to explain and to do that I need you to see the situation from my perspective. I'm not saying I was right or in any way justified. In fact, I know I owe you an apology for doubting you. But I want you to understand." She cleared her throat. "Maybe then you can forgive me."

He gave a jerky nod and she continued.

"My stomach was still pouchy and I definitely was not looking or feeling my best. Breanna was wearing a fitted skirt and had these legs that looked like they should be on a Rockette." Reese shook her head at the memory and sighed. "When she smiled at something you said, she had the most perfect white teeth I'd ever seen."

"She's an attractive woman." He shrugged.

"She's more than attractive. She's... beautiful."

"*You're* beautiful."

"I wasn't feeling very beautiful. And there was Breanna, with a degree from Harvard and wearing a suit by one of your mother's favorite designers." Reese shook her head. "God, Duncan, your mother would love her. Louise would approve of her and *her people* in a minute. And your dad would be in heaven. She went to his alma mater."

"So because my parents would like her you decided I must be having an affair?"

She swallowed. As bad as foolish, he made her sound fickle. And so she reminded him, "It wasn't long after that that you began working late. You were hardly ever home.

When you were, we didn't talk and…" She motioned with her hand. "And then you started sleeping in the room down the hall."

"What choice did I have? You were sad all the time and so damned moody. You didn't want me to touch you." He paced to the table and sank sideways onto one of the chairs. "God, Reese, whenever I tried to make love to you, you pulled away. It was like, if you couldn't be a mother, you didn't want to be a wife, either. Do you have any idea how that made me feel?"

She hadn't then, but she did now. The pain was there, etched onto his handsome face. "I'm so sorry, Duncan."

"You weren't…interested in me anymore. It was like you'd fallen out of love with me."

"No." She went to him, stopping just inside the V of his legs and cupped his face. "That wasn't it. I promise you, that wasn't it at all. I've never fallen out of love with you."

His voice turned hoarse. "Then what? Why?"

"I don't…" But then her gaze dropped to her stomach and she recalled how she'd used to stand under the shower spray, trace the small scars on her belly from the laparoscopies and cry. "I didn't feel desirable or sexy or even confident in myself as a woman any longer. Instead I just felt...I just felt defective."

The confession didn't only startle Duncan, it shook Reese as well. She covered her mouth with one hand, but a sob escaped anyway.

"Hey." He stood, rubbed his hands up her arms. "Hey, don't do that. Don't cry, okay?"

But her eyes had already filled with tears that spilled right along with the words that had finally been freed from her subconscious.

"My body didn't just betray me, it betrayed you. It was keeping you from becoming a father. I hated myself for that."

"I was still your husband, Reese. That was enough for me."

"Was it?"

"Yes."

"But for how long? I saw the window of opportunity closing with each year that passed and I guess I got a little panicky, especially since whenever I brought up adoption you all but tuned me out."

He closed his eyes. "You're right. I did, but you tuned me out, too. What I wanted, what I thought, none of that seemed to matter to you."

She nodded miserably. "It wasn't that it didn't matter to me. I was just so sick of hormone injections and cycle charts and doctor appointments. I had to keep taking time off from work and then there were the fights with the insurance company to cover certain things." Of course, she and Duncan had borne most of the cost themselves, tens of thousands of dollars that in the end had bought them only heartache. "I just couldn't take any more."

"And I wanted to keep going," he said ruefully.

"It was such a roller coaster."

"God, I know. We'd be up one minute and plummeting down the next."

"And then we lost the babies."

They were both quiet for a moment.

"That was a really dark time," he said at last.

"The darkest. I felt like I'd been pitched over a cliff," she whispered. "But I never hit the bottom. I just kept falling and praying for a parachute. I felt so lost, so empty."

"Me, too,"

"But you didn't cry." Even now, as tears streaked down her face, his eyes were dry. "You just…you just went on with your life like nothing had happened."

"What else could I do? You were so devastated. One of us had to pick up the pieces."

"But I wanted us to grieve together."

He brushed away her tears now. "I thought you needed me to be strong."

"No. I just needed you to be there."

He took her hands in his, kissed the backs of them. "You'll never know how much I've regretted that I couldn't fix things for us."

"I never expected you to fix anything, Duncan. Honestly. I never blamed you for our situation. God, how could I? Sometimes I felt so guilty. I'm the one with the problem."

She'd said that before, and moments earlier she'd used the term defective. Why was it, he wondered, that he'd never realized just how much it had bothered her? How much it had hacked at her self-esteem and, as a result, at the very fabric of their marriage.

"I never saw it that way," he assured her. "It was *our* problem, Reese. Something we needed to tackle together."

"But we didn't tackle it together."

"No."

"We became separate and isolated from one another. Sometimes I felt so alone, Duncan. You used to tell me everything and then you just stopped sharing your feelings. You didn't want to talk about what was happening."

"I had a hard time accepting it, I guess. And when I did open up—"

"I didn't listen," Reese admitted.

"I had so many doubts, so many questions, especially when it came to adopting, and I didn't feel I could confide them in anyone."

"I'm sorry for that. So sorry," she told him. "It was selfish of me, but I guess I thought that eventually you would change your mind about adoption."

Change his mind?

His eyes did fill with tears now as he thought of what he had almost lost in his blindness.

"Duncan?"

"I told you a long time ago that I didn't know if I could love a baby that wasn't mine. I didn't get it. I didn't understand that as soon as I held Daniel, he would be mine in all the ways that really matter. It happened that fast, even though I've spent these past weeks denying it. I love him, Reese."

"Oh, Duncan."

"I want a chance to be his dad. And I want another chance to be your husband."

"I want a second chance, too."

"I love you."

"I love you, too," Reese said as she pulled him close.

They cried in each other's arms, finally grieving the past as a couple even as they celebrated the future.

They slept together that night, legs twined, bodies sated. They'd made love with tender sweetness before Daniel awoke from his nap, needing a fresh diaper and eager for some more formula. Duncan insisted on taking care of both needs. Reese had been only too happy to let him.

Late that night, when the house was dark

and quiet, they'd made love again. The passion infertility had robbed them of finally seemed to be restored or maybe it was just their fresh outlook that brought back the magic.

It was just after three in the morning when the sound of the baby's fussing roused Reese from sleep, but then Daniel quieted down again. When she rolled to her side to snuggle up against Duncan, he was gone. Over the baby monitor came the rhythmic creak of the rocking chair and the deep hum of a man's voice.

She tiptoed down the hall, peered around the doorjamb into the nursery. Duncan sat in the rocker, the baby resting against his broad chest. He was patting Daniel's small back and explaining baseball's designated hitter rule.

The corners of his mouth lifted when he saw her. "I've wanted to do this every night."

"Tell him about the nation's pastime?"

"No. Just hold him."

"He feels perfect, doesn't he?"

Duncan nodded, held out an arm to her. "That's because he is."

EPILOGUE

REESE beamed as she and Duncan, who held Daniel, stood before the judge in family court. Today their adoption was being made final. Today, the baby would officially and irrevocably become their son.

In honor of the occasion, Daniel wore a little charcoal suit identical to the one his father was wearing. Reese had on a brightly flowered dress that Louise had informed her beforehand that she didn't think was conservative enough to wear in a court of law. Reese had only smiled, and then ignored her mother-in-law's comment that she also should have straightened her hair into a more sophisticated style.

Reese knew the two women would never see eye to eye on much of anything—except for Daniel. They both agreed he was most beautiful, perfect. And they both loved Duncan and were happy he was finally happy as well.

Daniel was in Duncan's arms, drooling, babbling, laughing. At nearly ten months old he had five teeth and a crop of curling brown hair that was every bit as unmanageable as his mother's. He was crawling, pulling himself up on the furniture and every now and then he took a tentative step before falling on his diapered bottom. He also was saying a couple of words: Da-da, which he'd learned first to Duncan's delight. And Mama, which he called over and over again when he couldn't sleep at night. Even so, the word remained music to Reese's ears.

On this day, assorted relatives and friends filled the first two rows of Judge Horton's courtroom. They were there to witness the official making of a new family. Reese, of course, knew they had officially become a family that day at the grocery store when Duncan had called Daniel his son.

Reese's parents had flown in from Boston, and so had her sister and brother-in-law and their own bundle of joy now stirred in

Rochelle's arms. Her sister had delivered a boy two weeks after Reese's baby shower. The family joke was that Daniel looked far more like Reese than baby Kyle resembled Rochelle.

Sara held the video camera, its lens trained on the Newcastles, recording their joy as the judge made his pronouncement.

"The court is pleased to present, Daniel Ryan Newcastle, son of Duncan and Reese Newcastle."

Happy tears were shed and despite the venue, applause erupted. Even the judge joined in.

"Well, he's yours for good now," Jenny said afterward as she leaned over to give Reese a hug. "I don't think I've ever seen you and Duncan look happier. Babies are a very special gift."

Reese smiled at husband and then at the child he held with such obvious affection.

"None more so than this one," she agreed.

* * * * *

Turn the page for a sneak preview of
IF I'D NEVER KNOWN YOUR LOVE
by
Georgia Bockoven

From the brand-new series
Harlequin Everlasting Love
Every great love has a story to tell.™

One year, five months and four days missing

There's no way for you to know this, Evan, but I haven't written to you for a few months. Actually, it's been almost a year. I had a hard time picking up a pen once more after we paid the second ransom and then received a letter saying it wasn't enough. I was so sure you were coming home that I took the kids along to Bogotá so they could fly home with you and me, something I swore I'd never do. I've fallen in love with Colombia and the people who've opened their hearts to me. But fear is a constant companion when I'm there. I won't ever expose our children to that kind of danger again.

I'm at a loss over what to do anymore, Evan. I've begged and pleaded and thrown temper tantrums with every official I can corner both here and at home. They've been incredibly tolerant and understanding, but in the end as ineffectual as the rest of us.

I try to imagine what your life is like now, what you do every day, what you're wearing, what you eat. I want to believe that the people who have you are misguided yet kind, that they treat you well. It's how I survive day to day. To think of you being mistreated hurts too much. If I picture you locked away somewhere and suffering, a weight descends on me that makes it almost impossible to get out of bed in the morning.

Your captors surely know you by now. They have to recognize what a good man you are. I imagine you working with their children, telling them that you have children, too, showing them the pictures you carry in your wallet. Can't the men who have you understand how much your children miss you? How can it not matter to them?

How can they keep you away from us all this time? Over and over, we've done what they asked. Are they oblivious to the depth of their cruelty? What kind of people are they that they don't care?

I used to keep a calendar beside our bed next to the peach rose you picked for me before you left. Every night I marked another day, counting how many you'd been gone. I don't do that any longer. I don't want to be reminded of all the days we'll never get back.

When I can't sleep at night, I tell you about my day. I imagine you hearing me and smiling over the details that make up my life now. I never tell you how defeated I feel at moments or how hard I work to hide it from everyone for fear they will see it as a reason to stop believing you are coming home to us.

And I couldn't tell you about the lump I found in my breast and how difficult it was going through all the tests without you here to lean on. The lump was benign—the process reaching that diagnosis utterly terrifying. I couldn't stop thinking about what would happen to Shelly and Jason if something happened to me.

We need you to come home.

I'm worn down with missing you.

I'm going to read this tomorrow and will probably tear it up or burn it in the fireplace. I don't want you to get the idea I ever doubted what I was doing to free you or thought the work a burden. I would gladly spend the rest of my life at it, even if, in the end, we only had one day together.

You are my life, Evan.

I will love you forever.

★ ★ ★ ★ ★

*Don't miss this deeply moving
Harlequin Everlasting Love story about a
woman's struggle to bring back her kid-
napped husband from Colombia and her
turmoil over whether to let go, finally, and
welcome another man into her life.
IF I'D NEVER KNOWN YOUR LOVE
by Georgia Bockoven
is available March 27, 2007.*

*And also look for
THE NIGHT WE MET
by Tara Taylor Quinn,
a story about finding love
when you least expect it.*

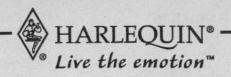

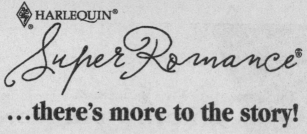
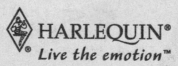

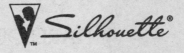

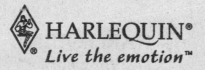

HARLEQUIN®
INTRIGUE®

BREATHTAKING ROMANTIC SUSPENSE

Shared dangers and passions lead to electrifying romance and heart-stopping suspense!

Every month, you'll meet six new heroes who are guaranteed to make your spine tingle and your pulse pound. With them you'll enter into the exciting world of Harlequin Intrigue— where your life is on the line and so is your heart!

THAT'S INTRIGUE— ROMANTIC SUSPENSE AT ITS BEST!

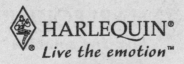